BEAUTIFUL DEFIANCE

CAMBRIDGE HIGH MAYHEM

ASHLYN MATHEWS

Cover design by Melissa Gill Designs

Edited by Courtney Umphress

Beautiful Defiance/Ashlyn Mathews. -- 1st ed.

❀ Created with Vellum

"Her heart was wild, but I didn't want to catch it. I wanted to run with it to set mine free."

~ Atticus

I disliked him the moment I saw him on that first day of school. He is everything I detest in a guy. Arrogance. Power. *Influence.* An ego the size of the Pacific Ocean.

Seven Shanahan is all of that and more with the cocky smirk on his face and the way he struts down the hall, flanked by his friends. He and his friends Trace and Malice are gods at Cambridge High, where ninety percent of the student body is loaded.

Well, their parents are, anyway.

Trust fund kids. Spoiled. *Impressionable.* Tolerant of the jerks at the top of the food chain. Seven and his friends keep everyone in line from their perch, wearing their black-and-yellow letterman jackets as a symbol of their high school royalty status.

From my vantage point behind the open door of my locker, I sneak a glance at the stars of Cambridge High's football team, Mayhem. Seven Shanahan, quarterback. Trace Saints, wide receiver. Malice Sterling, offensive lineman.

The guys are similar in looks, with their chiseled jawlines, dark tousled hair under their backward baseball caps, and intense eyes framed by thick brows and fringed with long lashes that could give any girl lash envy. They are also equal in height, six feet, give or take a half inch.

Seven and Trace are lean but not lanky. Their clothes mold to their bodies like a second skin, showcasing their wide shoulders, muscular arms, broad chests, and washboard abs. Malice fits his lineman position. He is bulk and muscle, a human bulldozer.

The jockholes are a photographer's cover model dream come true. It's a shame the "model" part doesn't extend to their behavior. Be different from them or challenge their established social hierarchy, and there's a guarantee you'll be public enemy number one.

I hold my textbooks to my chest and close my locker.

No matter which high school I'm sent to, the

halls are chocked full of the same cliques. Jocks. Nerds. Stoners. Gang bangers. It's so universal, it's laughable. There are also the same kinds of guys and girls. Nice. Mean. Smart. Funny. Blessed with good looks, or not.

Seven and his teammates amble down the hall toward me. I look away but too late, my resting bitch face catches Seven's attention.

"What you staring at, Safari?" he sneers.

Safari? Okay, I can see how he's interpreting my outfit as such. There's a red bandana around my neck, tied at the ends. And I'm wearing a buttoned-up, long-sleeved white shirt half-tucked into tiki brown cargo pants. Not to mention my boots are professional grade—sturdy, leather, and steel-toed.

"Nothing. I'm looking at nothing." I blow at the nails I've painted a mustard yellow. The color clashes nicely with my favorite shade of lipstick—Fatal Plum.

He looks me up and down and flashes straight white teeth, his sneer doing nothing to lessen how good-looking he is in this confusing mix of menacing and holy hotness kind of way. I swear the girls loitering nearby sigh with longing.

"Did you peg me as a nobody?"

The conversation around us stops. The other

students stare. My stomach knots. If we weren't on full display, I'd run for the nearest bathroom and hurl my breakfast into the garbage bin.

But we are the center of attention, and I can't waver. If I show an ounce of weakness, I'll give a jerk like Seven the power to hurt me. I'm done with hurting. What I'm not done with is putting up a brave front and fighting an equal grounds fight.

"You're a good-for-nothing nobody." I make it clear what I think of him and his you're-dirt-beneath-my-expensive-sneakers attitude.

Boys like Seven and his friends are a dime a dozen where I grew up until the mention of a paternity suit landed me in the rich farm town of Cambridge, Washington.

Here, away from the housing developments and the sly grins of my foster brothers, I can spread my wings, inhale the crisp, clean air, and find purpose for my existence.

Now, I just need to extract myself from the crosshairs of Seven Shanahan's attentions. Damn it, I should have looked away quicker. We are two weeks into the school year, and from the hardened gleam in his dark-as-coal eyes, he plans on punishing me for mouthing off.

I'm right. He leans in and whispers near my ear,

"Watch your back, Safari. I'll take a chunk out of you if you're not careful."

I'm on the edge of clucking my tongue and sassing him, but for the sake of not calling further attention to myself, I shrug and shove past him and his friends. I expect him to punish me, but not so soon.

He sticks out his foot. I trip and fall forward, landing on my hands and knees. Books go flying. Papers fall from my notebook. Male laughter echoes off the walls. I glance over my shoulder and glare at him, refusing to wince or cry out in pain. He rolls his eyes and mimes giving a blowjob.

I grit my teeth. So be it. *Seven Shanahan, this means war.*

2

SEVEN

I don't feel bad for knocking the new girl down a peg. Girls with attitude and hateful glares aren't welcome on me and my boys' turf. What we like is what I see waiting at the end of the hall.

A group of girls eye us expectantly. I run my gaze over their fine bodies. Their hair is in my favorite shades. Burnt caramel. Dark chocolate. Honey blonde. Platinum blonde. Fiery red. But not pitch black. Black is death.

Their skin is pale and smooth, unlike the girl from earlier with the natural tan. Blue eyes. Green eyes. Dark-brown eyes. Not clear amber like hers. The girls direct their flirty smiles our way. Predictable. So is the lust in their eyes. They want a piece of us. Our mouths on theirs. Our hands on their bodies.

Soon enough, ladies. There's a party at my place tonight, the folks gone for the week for their millionth try at saving their marriage.

"Hi there, Seven."

Hannah walks over and runs her manicured finger up and down my arm, sending hot need to my junk. I stop her fiery caresses and grasp her hand in mine. She has other ideas. Fully aware of all eyes on us, she takes my hand and sucks on my middle finger.

Her tongue on my finger, her wet, warm mouth . . . I groan and resist the urge to stroke my cock through my jeans. Fuck sakes, this girl is killing me softly and slowly with how well she sucks my damn finger.

"Hannah." Jesus, I'm panting.

She lets go of my finger and, biting down on her smile, says, "Tonight. You and me."

How can I refuse? I nod, too turned on to speak. My boys and I, we head to our class. They shove me back and forth with shit-eating grins on their faces. They understand I've been wanting in Hannah's pants, but you see, she has a mean-as-fuck older brother who likes to keep a close eye on his fine-ass little sis.

But the dude's away at college. And that, my friends, give me free rein to do whatever the hell I want with Hannah.

In math class, I sit behind the new girl. Her long black hair drapes over the back of her chair, the strands falling over her white shirt like muddied waters after a flash storm.

To show her not to mess with me, that I'm a somebody and she's the nobody, I shove my shoe into the small of her back, leaving a muddy imprint on her shirt. It rained buckets, and the walk from the school parking lot to the front doors was fraught with puddles.

She doesn't flinch or acknowledge that my shoe is pushing into her back so hard, I can feel her rigid spine straight to my core. I press harder. She picks up her desk and scoots forward. I scoot after her. The guys notice and snicker. The teacher turns from writing a math problem on the board and lifts a drawn on brow.

Mrs. Bowman glances around the room and zones in on the new girl. Her desk isn't lined up with the others, and Mrs. Bowman notices. Another smirk lights up my face the instant I see the annoyance on hers. I had Mrs. Bowman for math last year, too, and the thing is, she's particular and hates when things are askew.

"Miss Kim, please scoot your desk back and center it with the desk in front of you, please."

What will New Girl do? My body pulls taut with anticipation

"I'm sorry, Mrs. Bowman, but I can't see the board very well. I forgot my glasses at home."

Mrs. Bowman, who is wearing glasses, well, damn it, her face softens.

"Oh, dear, that's a problem. Why don't you and Allison switch seats?"

New Girl moves to the front of the classroom, and my ex-girlfriend takes her place.

"Allison, please scoot the chair back and line it up with the one in front of you."

Allison does as the teacher asks. When Mrs. Bowman returns to solving the problem on the board, Allison glances over her shoulder and shoots me a tentative smile. I look off to the side, avoiding the pleading in her big blue eyes. We broke up for a reason. I don't take well to cheaters. I also don't believe in second chances.

Most of all, I don't like people who disturb the

peace, and reek of rebellion and defiance. I stare a hole in the back of Safari's head.

Rebellion and defiance give someone the potential to unseat me and my boys from our thrones. Gives them the chance to pump back into my heart the metaphorical blood I lost when a girl ripped my heart in two.

Black hair. Amber eyes. She comes to me in my dreams and my nightmares, and every goddamn time, I wake up to the same ending no matter how hard I tried to change what happened that day.

In the end, the girl I tried to save dies.

3

My goddamn truck doesn't start, and I have a party to prep for. I kick the tire, then regret taking out my anger on the old girl. I bought the red Chevy Silverado truck with money earned from doing odd jobs in the nearby town of McMillan.

Sure, my old man is loaded, but there's satisfaction in hard work and making my way in life without my dad's handed-down wealth.

"Hey, man, we gotta move our asses." Trace clamps his meaty paw on my shoulder and squeezes. Malice, the fucker, plows into me from behind, and I stumble toward his damn sportscar.

"We ain't gonna all fit in your pansy ass GT-R, bro." I shove my elbow in his gut. He grunts. "And why you gotta drive around in a one-hundred-thousand-dollar deathtrap? We live out in the boondocks. Who you trying to impress?"

He doesn't answer. Malice marches past me, and that's how I know I've hit a sensitive nerve. I hurry after him. It's not in me to pass up the chance of ribbing on him.

I shoot my truck a parting glance over my shoulder, making sure the old girl will be okay. She's one of a few vehicles left in the school's back parking lot.

Tomorrow, I'll hitch a ride with Trace. After practice, I'll figure out what the deal is with her. Maybe this time around, she's finally bit the dust. I shrug my backpack higher on my shoulder and cram my hands inside my pockets. It's my own damn fault for not taking better care of her. But with the shit that's been going on with my parents—the fighting, the accusations—I needed to do something with the anger swirling inside me.

That something is working out like crazy and partying. Yeah, lots and lots of partying since school started. My parents' arguments have spilled over from summer into the school year, and the uncertainty of where I'll be months from now is fucking with my A-game on and off the field.

"Dude, don't tell me you're trying to impress Riley Lee? She ain't even here."

Riley worked for Malice's family before she moved to Dumas for school.

Malice yanks open the door, flips forward the front seat, and throws his thumb at the back seat. I shake my head.

"I'm riding shotgun."

"No go. You brought up Riley, and that earns you a spot sitting with your knees to your heartless chest."

I put my palms up. "You need to forget her. One, she'll graduate *from college* the same year we finish *high school*. Two, she was Midnight's girl first, and when your cousin digs his claws into a girl, he doesn't let her go. Not someone as different as Riley."

Different isn't the best word to describe Riley Lee. But I can't well accuse the girl Malice has a hard-on for as being untrustworthy and a troublemaker of the worst kind.

Riley is one of those girls a guy wants to kiss senseless *and* ream out at the same time for her defiance and recklessness. Her sister, Rue, is cut from the same cloth, except Rue's defiance and recklessness are on the down low, quiet and lethal.

"Forget her. There are other girls more than willing to fuck with your head. Bonus? They'll let you wet your dick too."

I'm not kidding either. The girls go gaga for Malice, with his unpredictable moods and hooded I-couldn't-give-a-flying-fuck eyes.

The guy's always angry. I don't get why. Dude's loaded, has his pick of girls, and lives in his own place on his parents' property.

"Let the poor girl go. Otherwise, Midnight will kick your ass to kingdom come for entertaining the idea of going after his woman."

Thank fuck he comes to his senses, mumbling something to the effect of, "Yeah, can't have discord in the family."

Family is everything to Malice. Same goes for me. I squeeze into the back seat, and clamping my hands on my boys' shoulders, I give them the four-one-one on the girls coming to the party tonight.

"Super fly. Super fine. The best of the best for us, bros. There'll be no defiance. No rebellion. The girls will fall in line and do whatever the fuck we want them to."

Trace and Malice smile big. Predictable and obedience off the field means more mayhem on the football field. It's what we're known for. For shitting on our opponents to the point the game is lopsided with how high into the stratosphere the score is.

I throw. Malice has my back. Trace catches my throws and runs the ball into the endzone. We pound our opponents into submission because you see, I am the king of the game, and this king will not be unseated from his throne.

No one will overthrow my kingdom, including the five-foot-five straight-as-a-board pissed-off new girl with her defiance.

4

*T*he house is dark. The estate is quiet. Inside my bedroom, I change into a one-piece swimsuit that covers the scars across my back.

There might not ever be a chance like this again to sample the heated pool. Hannah is at Seven's party. (Who has a party on a Tuesday?). Henry is away at college. And the Stevensons are on an island somewhere, celebrating their wedding anniversary.

Though no one's around, I close the door of the small guesthouse in the back of the two-story mansion with a soft click. After I secure the housekey to my tennis shoes using the shoelaces, I get a running start and bolt up the hillside.

What will it be like to swim on my back and stare up at the star-filled sky? I'll know soon. At the top of the hill, I practically skip to the gate that surrounds the pool. I unlock it and set my towel on a lounge chair. Steam rises from the water.

I slide off my shoes. Goosebumps dot my skin. I hug myself and rub at my arms, my stomach suddenly in knots.

There's no harm in going for a swim. I'm a great swimmer, so that's not the problem. The issue is being disobedient for selfish reasons, partaking in Thomas's extravagance. A heated pool. A mansion on five acres. Gated entrance. Five-car garage.

I don't fit in, and I doubt I ever will.

The urge to rebel is a difficult habit to break. It wasn't always this way.

After my parents' deaths, I listened and obeyed, hoping my obedience would bring them back to life and they'd take me away from the loneliness and the misery of never being wanted for who I am.

But no amount of obedience brought them back, and I returned to what I know how best to do. Defy.

To defy is to be punished, and punishment brings about a pain that teaches me life is pain. Pain is an escape from the numbness of life living in foster homes and being reliant on others' show of mercy.

Tired of thinking of my past when I have my future to think of, I walk over to the deep end of the pool and dive in. That first splash of warm water on my cool skin is like biting into a hotteok straight off the pan. Or spooning a mouthful of warm apple pie dripping with cinnamon and whipped cream into my mouth. Pure heaven.

Closing my eyes and holding my breath, I cross my arms, crisscross my legs, and sink to the bottom. Pieces of my hair caress my face like a wispy breeze. I turn my head side to side. If anyone were to dive in after me, they'd see an impish grin on my face. I stay under the water until my chest is ready to explode.

I come up for air and swim laps from one end of the pool to the other, first on my back, then with my face in and out of the water, the strokes precise from my early years of swim lessons at the YMCA.

When I'm happy and out of breath, I push off the side of the pool and swim on my back. The stars wink at me, and the moon plays hide and seek behind the clouds.

Goodness, it's so beautiful. I glide across the pool and concentrate on the sounds around me. Frogs croaking. Crickets chirping. Mating calls?

My face heats. I mean, why else would animals make noises in the night other than for booty? Sticking that thought in the recesses of my mind, I hum a tune. "Rewrite the Stars," by Zac Efron and Zendaya from the movie *The Greatest Showman.*

Priceless staring up at the stars. Having the place to myself. Not having to worry that I'll be attacked in my sleep. Or beat for doing something that is wrong in someone else's opinion but right in every way to me.

I cherish the silence like it's my last night on this earth. I listen to the frogs and the crickets and brand their little melodies to memory. Also brand into my memory the wrinkles on my fingertips from staying so long in the pool.

Not wanting to be one big raisin, I swim to the ladder at the end of the pool closest to the house. A noise from the front of the house sends tingles of apprehension up and down my spine.

Is Hannah home early? Shit, she'll tell Thomas I swam in their precious pool, and he'll scold me for not making sure someone was around to keep an eye on me.

Thomas is a liar and a cheater, but for the most part, he's a decent guy if you can overlook the lying and the cheating. I hurry to the ladder. Masculine laughter echoes in the night. There's not one guy but four guys. I bolt for the ladder.

Water splashes around me. I grit my teeth. In the

end, the racket I made didn't matter. The guys heading my way already have it in their minds to enjoy the pool too.

They're in their swim trunks with towels draped over their shoulders. Groaning, I shove away from the ladder and swim to the opposite side. Before I can get out, the guys circle the pool. They're like great white sharks scenting blood in the water. Too bad I won't be easy prey. I swim to the middle of the pool.

"Leigh. Funny seeing you here." Henry sticks his foot into the pool and kicks, splashing me in the face.

"You too." I blink away the water in my eyes. "Thomas said you would only be home on holidays and long breaks."

Something to do with wanting to immerse himself in the college experience is how Thomas explained why his only son wouldn't be making the one-hour drive home on the weekends. Henry stuck around Cambridge long enough to meet me before he left for Dumas. He followed me and his dad around the estate, a silent and brooding shadow behind us, as Thomas gave me a tour of the grounds.

Thomas pointed to the places I could go and what is off-limits, including Seven's parents' place on the other side of the low-lying fence. The Shanahans are private people.

"*My dad* knows jack shit."

"Did they kick you out of DU? Sent you back home to live with Daddy Dearest?"

Henry is a younger version of his dad. Dirty-blond hair. Square jawline. Expressive hazel eyes. Some would say they are classically handsome.

"Why are you here, Leigh?" He lowers himself onto the edge of the pool and sits. His friends do the same.

"It's none of your business." Tipping my chin, I move my arms back and forth, the strokes long and even. Inside, I am a mess of nerves. I should play nice. I can't win this war of wills when my arms are getting tired. Soon, my legs will cramp up.

"You're a stranger. A nobody. Why the hell did my father move you here?"

"You should ask *Thomas.*"

"Already did. He refuses to tell."

"Then respect his decision. What he and I have is private."

"What you and he have?" He glances in the direction of the guesthouse.

"The place isn't yours anymore. Thomas made it clear it's my space now."

He points a thick finger at me. "If you're sleeping with my father, I'm gonna make you regret you were ever born, Leigh."

Huh? And gross! "As if. The Stevenson dick isn't good enough for me."

I pushed too far. Henry's growl pierces the air. He launches his body at me. I rush to the opposite end of the pool. There is splashing behind me. Crap!

I scramble up the ladder and am about to make a clean getaway, but someone grabs ahold of my ankle and yanks me into the pool. My chin hits the ladder rung. I bite down on my tongue. Metallic taste in my mouth. I would spit, but I don't want to get my blood in Thomas's pristine pool.

"Fucking take back what you said, Leigh."

I would but he's dunking my head underwater. I claw at his hands. He doesn't let up. I open my eyes. The chlorine burns them. I shake my head, trying to free myself from his grip, but he has a firm grasp on my hair. I slam my feet on his thighs and push off, but his fingers hold on to me by the front of my swimsuit, keeping me from making much leeway backward.

My vision goes in and out. My chest collapses onto itself.

This is it. Eighteen years of living going down the

drain because I'd rather defy than admit the truth of what Thomas is to me.

I close my eyes and pray for my defiant soul. Hear yelling from a distance. Are my parents fighting in heaven? God, can they quit it? Fingers fist in my hair and yank my head out of the water. Large hands grab me under my arms and tug the rest of my body out of the pool. I sputter. Gulp air. Cough in fits.

Is Hannah home? Did she rescue me from Henry and the chip on his shoulder? I open my eyes and stare up into the blackest eyes I've ever seen.

"Oh, crap, I've died and gone to hell."

The devil sneers at me. "And payback's a bitch, Safari. You're in my debt now for saving your ass."

I glance off to the side, where there's a commotion and yelling. Seven's friends and Henry's are holding Henry at bay. No doubt Henry wants to have another go at me. He'll have to stand in line behind Seven.

I push myself into a sitting position. The world spins. I groan. Suddenly, my world shifts again. Seven picks me up off the ground and carries me to the front door. I give him the bad news.

"I'm staying at the guesthouse in the back."

"Like in the waaay back?"

"Yes. Put me down. I'm too heavy."

He scoffs. "Don't think you can bolt. I'll catch you every time."

I should be put off by the idea of him chasing after me like I'm a criminal. Instead, a thrill passes through me. I push the unexpected excitement down, chalking it up to the traumatic experience of my near-drowning.

"I don't plan on running off." There's nowhere to go. I also like eating three square meals a day for a change.

"Good. Do me a favor? Grab your shoes. We'll need the house key." He tips me to the ground.

I'm not having it. "Put me down and go back to your friends. I don't want to keep you guys from partying the night away."

"They can wait the fuck until I'm good and ready for all I care."

Eloquent response. And . . . the king has spoken. The knights of his court won't leave until their leader returns. What will happen if his friends ever say no? I'm guessing they won't. From what I've seen, Seven's friends are loyal. I envy him that. I never stuck around one place long enough to make friends.

Sighing, I grab my shoes and being careful not to

smack him with them, I curl my arms around his neck.

"When will that be?" I say into his hair.

"When you and I are done discussing the rules and the boundaries for your time in Cambridge."

Ah, so that's the kind of talk we'll be having at the end of this *wonderful* night.

"Don't you want to return to your party sooner rather than later? Think of all the 'action' you're missing out on."

"There's no missing out going on. Party didn't happen. My parents cut their trip short."

His jaw tightens. Had I not been so close, I would've missed the dead giveaway.

"Did they have fun?" I don't know why I asked. Maybe it's because he's put out that they came back early, and I want to further rejoice in his unhappiness. I hide my face in his hair. I'm a horrible person for thinking such mean thoughts.

"Don't much care. What matters is there's another party. That's where we were headed."

"You stopped by here. Why?"

"The party's at the lake, and seeing that Hannah's place is closest to mine and she's already drunk off her ass from starting early at a *different* party, she wanted my boys and I to grab swimsuits for her and her friends."

"You planned on breaking and entering?"

"Nah, I saw Henry driving up to the house. I figured my boys could distract him and his friends and I'd sneak inside."

"You know where Hannah's room is?"

There are five bedrooms and six bathrooms in the mansion.

"Doesn't every guy?"

I don't answer. I don't know Hannah.

"Imagine our surprise when we found Henry attempting to drown the live-in groundskeeper."

Live-in groundskeeper? Ha-ha. Except what Seven said isn't far from the truth. I don't plan on living off Thomas. I'll pitch in and do my share.

When Thomas showed me around the property, he dropped a tidbit that I grasped on to for dear life. Their long-time groundskeeper died recently. What if I take over that role?

I've asked the old guy who lives next door how to use the ride-on lawnmower. I also asked him to differentiate for me the weeds from the non-weeds scattered around Thomas's estate. When Thomas gets back from his trip, I'll run the idea by him. The worst thing he can say is, "Hell no."

"Isn't it too cold to be swimming in the lake?"

Seven walks us down the steep hillside. He's careful, his steps slow and steady, but the grass is wet. He slips. Righting himself, he jostles me closer to his body. I inhale a deep breath at our close call from tumbling down the hillside, and catch a whiff of Seven's scent. Cinnamon and the distinct smell of wet grass from today's earlier rainstorm.

"Should Hannah be near the water if she's drunk?"

My voice is steady. Inside, my lungs aren't expanding like they should with every breath I take. Seven and I are too close. The hair on his arm brushes my skin. His warm breath coasts over the shell of my ear.

It's unnerving having a guy this close to me. It's also unnerving how hyperaware my body is to his. I swear his heart beats in time to mine, and our breathing is in sync too.

And the way he's stroking my flesh above my knee . . . Jesus, I'm heating up from the inside out. Thank goodness we're at the guesthouse. I'm ready to pass out from the sheer torture of his fingertips on my sensitive skin.

He sets me on my feet. I let myself inside the guesthouse. To my annoyance, Seven follows me inside and plops down onto my couch. I look away from how well his shirt, wet from my swimsuit, clings to his skin.

"Who says anything about swimming?"

It hits me what they could be doing in their swimsuits. "Are you saying the girls wanted to parade in front of you guys in their bikinis?"

"Yeah. We boys would bid on the girls. Winner gets the girl. The girls get the money. A win-win."

"That's pathetic."

"To you."

"Demeaning too."

"And beauty pageants aren't? Or how about strip clubs? Or something like Thunder Down Under?"

"Thunder down what?"

He smirks. "It's like Magic Mike but Australian dudes in Vegas."

"No matter how magical or Outbackishly sexy they are, I wouldn't partake."

"Partake? Not interested in hot dudes? You're a prude. Or are you into girls?"

"Believe me, I'm into guys. And if I'm a prude because I don't believe sexuality should be flaunted, then okay, I'm a damn prude."

"If it's not looks and sexuality, then what is there to look forward to in a girl?"

Is this guy for real?

"Oh, I don't know, maybe someone to laugh and cry with. To share secrets and heartache with. To dream with. To argue with just to have some kissing and making up to do later. There are many reasons to want to spend time with someone."

"And obedience?"

I growl under my breath. This guy is off his rocker, having been hit in the head one too many times.

"Obedience is boring," I snap.

Obedience is silence, and my silence made it okay for a horrible guy to continue hurting my mother, holding power, influence, and his arrogance over her head.

"But if it's obedience you're wanting, you should practice what you preach. Word is you've been very disobedient. Partying. Not keeping up with your studies. Talking back to the coach. Picking fights on the field."

"Keeping tabs on me, huh, Leigh?"

He gets up off the couch and stalks toward me. I back up until I'm against the edge of the breakfast bar.

I cross my arms and tip my chin at him. "I don't keep tabs on anyone, so don't flatter yourself.

Everyone knows you've been short-tempered and distracted."

"Short-tempered and distracted?" He reaches out and snaps the strap on my swimsuit. "Should I be short-tempered and distracted by you, Leigh?"

Why does he have to say my name like that, with heat and something wicked? Like he wants a taste of me, licking me from head to toe before he takes a chunk out of me with his perfect, pearly white teeth?

"That's Safari to you." I push him out of the way and barge past him, ready to show him out.

He grabs me by the arm and swings me around. I collide into his chest. He grasps my chin and tilts my face up, forcing me to look him in the eye.

"Not so fast. You owe me for saving your life."

His gaze drops to my mouth. I twist out of his hold.

"Sorry, but I'm not in the business of owing anyone anything."

Bypassing the hard glint in his eyes and his clenched jaw, I grab my backpack off the floor, heave its weight to my chest, and shove it into his.

"The battery I took from your truck. Now, we're even."

"*H*ey, man, you all good here?"

I glance up from beneath the hood of my pickup truck. Malice and Trace are jogging toward me. I lower the hood and grab my backpack off the ground.

I cannot believe Leigh stole the fucking battery. When did she have the time, and most importantly, who the fuck helped her? The girls I know don't know their way around the inside of a truck, much less have the strength to cart off *in her backpack* a heavy-as-a-load-of-bricks truck battery.

"Hey, have you seen the new girl?"

"You should be asking yourself that," Trace says. "She was last seen with you."

We didn't make it to last night's party. Instead, I

straddled a lounge chair and stared a hole in Henry's face with my hands tented over my mouth while my friends and teammates shot the breeze with him and his friends about college life and college girls.

After I gave the order it was time to call it a night, they exchanged spank bank pictures and we left. Henry hasn't been far from my mind. I hate that asshole for messing with Leigh.

That job belongs to me. I reserve the right to let it be me and only me who makes Leigh's life miserable. However, if she drops her defiance, I'll forgive and forget, welcoming her to the town and my turf with open arms.

"It's still early. Doesn't she take the bus?" This from Malice.

"You noticed?" Shit, did I say that out loud?

He ignores my question and takes the conversation down a path that doesn't sit well with me for many reasons, the primary one being that he is onto something.

"Any girl who can rock a one-piece is mighty fine in my book. She leaves enough to the imagination, if you know what I mean."

I'm about to tell him to leave her the fuck alone. That he should return to getting a hard-on for Riley.

But the bus pulls into the parking lot. Malice cups the back of his neck and shoots me a sly grin.

"Waiting for your girl like a pussy-whipped mother-effer." He tsks.

A well-planted sock in the face is the cure for Malice's what-the-fuckery.

"She is not my girl."

"Then it shouldn't be a problem if *I* pursue her. You're right; it's time I get over Riley."

I see red. Turn so fast I get whiplash. I grab him by the front of his shirt. Slam my other hand, palm up, against the underside of his jaw.

"She's off limits."

He smirks. "We'll see about that." He untangles my fingers from his shirt. Smacks aside my palm.

We'll see about that? Where is his loyalty? Did he lose his grip on who sits firmly on the throne? Fuck's sake, my boys and I never fight over a girl.

My hands balled at my sides, I watch kids walk off the bus.

I'm not seeing Leigh. Is she okay? Don't know how long she was underwater before the guys and I jumped the fence and found Henry drowning her. Damn, the murderous glare on the asshole's face. What were he and Leigh disagreeing about?

"Anyone have her number?"

"Hannah might."

Thank fuck for Trace's ability to think on his feet.

We go in search of Hannah. As soon as she sees us, she stops talking, licks her lips, and does this weird shit with her eyes. Sorry, babe, but you are not pulling off the bedroom-eyes look. Hannah looks high. I cut to the chase.

"Haven't seen her." Hannah shuts her locker and pops her gum. "Not giving you her number either. Don't have it."

"She's living on your family's property."

"So? Only my dad has hired help's numbers."

"Your brother and his friends still hanging out at the house?"

"They drove back to Dumas this morning."

I unfurl my fists, not realizing my hands are balled at my sides. The first bell rings. Ten minutes before classes start. My boys rest their bodies on the lockers. They're not in a hurry. They're interested in how this new situation of my being interested in Leigh in a different way pans out.

Believe me, I'm not interested in Leigh other than to punish her for messing with what's mine. No one messes with my truck. The battery is what gives the old girl life. Leigh might wrongfully think we're even, but we're not. Not by a long shot.

"Look, Seven, she probably overslept and missed the bus. No need to worry, okay?"

Worry? Who's worrying?

"Not that I give a shit. I hate her. Well, gotta go." Her friends are tugging at her sleeves. "See you after school."

Hannah and the other cheerleaders hurry off to class. We look after them. Trace is predictable, his eyes glued on their asses. Malice though, he's not giving a flying fuck and that worries me.

It's time to shut down the search party.

"Come on, bros. Hannah's right. We shouldn't give a shit. New girl's defiance is nothing but trouble for us to squash and stomp on."

"Here, here."

Me and Trace fist bump. Malice is quiet. Then he does the unforgivable. He walks the fuck away. I growl under my breath. Curse his family for good measure too.

Not wasting more head space on my disloyal friend, I stomp to my first class. I make it through lunch before needing to grab cash from inside my locker for a kid who did a favor for me. I yank open the door.

Poof! A plume of mustard yellow and dark purple smacks me in the face. Powder coats my skin. I suck in a breath and inhale a mouthful of it. There is only one person stupid enough to take defiance to a new level. Nails painted yellow. Full lips in dark purple.

Leigh Kim.

I scrub my hand over my stained face.

I am going to wring her defiant neck.

6

SEVEN

I jump the sorry-of-an-excuse-for-a-fence separating the Stevenson's property and my parents' and stomp over to the guesthouse.

The curtains are drawn. I pound on the door. Nothing. I pound harder. Kick the door with the toes of my sneaker when there's still no answer.

On the second go at the door, it swings open. I barge inside Leigh's place, not giving a care that she's in her underwear and a tank top sans bra.

"Seven, what are you doing here? Shouldn't you be at school?"

She's staring at the floor. Damn right, she should be avoiding looking me in the eye. I'm so pissed off right now I'd scare the living daylights out of her.

"If it's about yesterday, I'm sorry I didn't thank you for saving my life."

Her words strip me of my anger. Goddammit, how can she defuse the situation so easily with her crappy-ass words? She glances up and sees what is smeared on my face. Her eyes widen. She sucks in a breath.

I'm doing the same. See red too. Her bottom lip is swollen and cut up. There's a scrape on her right temple, the skin red and puckered. I grasp her by the jaw.

"Who the fuck did this? Was it Henry?"

She doesn't answer. No shit she doesn't. What I'm quickly learning is Leigh isn't like the other girls. She isn't compliant. Moldable. Predictable. Leigh is defiant, what I don't want in my life. Defiance is dangerous.

"Why didn't you wash this off?" She reaches out and fans her fingers on my skin.

"I was too pissed," I grumble, resisting the impulse to cover her hand with mine. To beg for her to dig her fingertips into my flesh. To help me feel something other than the emptiness that's lived in me since I was fifteen.

Jesus H. Christ, her fingers on my skin are like that first and last warm breeze of summer, heralding the change in seasons. I mentally shake off that thought. Fuck's sake, I'm waxing poetry and all because a girl touched my face.

I step back, hoping she'll get the message and stop touching me. If she did, she's not listening.

Again, why did I believe Leigh would listen to a word or any nonverbal cue I gave her?

"It's just cornstarch, silly."

"*Silly?*"

"Tough guy?" A shrug and a tentative smile from her.

"That's better." I smile back.

Wait, the fuck? Are we *flirting*? Her fingers fall from my face, and she goes to the kitchen, returning with a damp cloth.

I mutter, "Thanks," grab the cloth from her, and scrub off the *cornstarch*. "You didn't answer my question, Leigh."

"It's none of your business." She takes the cloth from me and tosses it into the washing machine. "I'm sorry for the prank. I set it up before you saved my life."

She sinks onto the couch like dead weight. Am I missing something, or did Leigh sway?

"Leigh, are you okay? Are you in trouble?"

If she is, I'll get her out of it *after* I pummel

whoever messed with her beautiful face. Leigh Kim. Beautiful. Defiance. Beautiful Defiance. Fits her.

"Everything's fine. Go back to school already. You, we, everyone at Cambridge, can't afford for you to miss a game because your grades are in the shitter."

In the shitter? This girl and her mouth. She rests her head in her palms, shoves her fingers in her hair, and shakes out the inky strands. Her defiance is like a damn rock in my shoe, but Leigh looking worn down? It's annoying as fuck that I care.

"I'm not leaving until you look me in the eye and tell me to piss off."

Her fingers slide out of her hair. She rests her elbows on her knees, lifts her head, and tells me to piss off. I take a good look at her. Her cheeks are flushed, and not in a I'm-turned-the-fuck-on-by-you pink, but in a I'm-running-a-fever shade of crimson. I get down on my haunches in front of her and place the back of my hand on her forehead.

"You're burning up."

"No shit, Sherlock."

"Leigh, this isn't the time to be defiant."

"It's not defiance. I'm being a sarcastic smart-ass."

"Hey, watch the language."

"Hypocrisy doesn't suit you, Seven."

"Fuck's sake, Leigh, you're sick. Probably swallowed cum-filled, pissed-in pool water."

"Gross." She wiggles her nose, looking adorable as fuck.

"Just saying."

"Cum-filled, pissed-in pool aside, I'm fine. Go. Be gone. Piss off." She shoves me away and flops onto her stomach on the couch, her face smushed into the cushion.

I'm ready to rip into her and either demand she tell me who fucked up her face or ask what she needs at the store that'll help her feel better. Except I see what's giving her the fever.

On the back of her thigh is a long gash. The skin is red and angry. I skim my finger over the cut. She smacks at me.

"Hurt, didn't it?"

"Yes."

"Leigh, we need to get you to the hospital. There's a festering infection on the back of your leg."

"Don't want to go."

"Sorry, Defiance, but you don't get a say in this."

I help her to a sitting position. Help her poke her arms through the sleeves of her baggy sweatshirt and stick her skinny legs into a pair of sweatpants, too, that I found inside her bedroom.

After I slide her feet into her tennis shoes, I grab her by the waist, pull her up, and tug the sweatpants up until they're hanging loose on her hips. Her head falls onto my shoulder. Her arms curl around my waist.

"Seven, I don't feel good."

"I bet you don't." I pick her up and hold her close to my body. "Don't worry. The doctors and nurses will get you feeling better in no time. They'll pump you full of miracle antibiotics and kill that mean-ass infection."

"You've been sick like this too?"

"Yeah. Junior year, I was running after this kid and hit my knuckles hard on the side of this dude's old truck. Split the skin. Rust got into the cut, and my body did not like that shit. My hand swelled up like a helium balloon."

"Nice analogy." Her hand settles on the spot over my heart. She gives me a pat. It's like we're old friends or something.

"Thanks," I mumble.

"Seven, why were you running after the poor kid?"

"He stole this old lady's purse. Knocked her the fuck over."

"Did you get back her purse?"

"Yeah. Yeah, I did. Punched the kid in the face with the knuckles that weren't cracked open."

"That's nice of you, Seven. You're her hero."

"I did what any decent human being would do."

"Where I grew up, the kids would have pilfered her purse down to the zipper and the lining."

"That's pathetic."

"It is."

"Are you glad you left?"

"Very. I don't miss any part of my old life."

"Nothing at all?"

"There is this one guy. He kept me out of trouble. Lately, he's too busy to pay me attention. A good thing. He can be a major pain in my ass."

"That so?"

She smiles. "So."

"He must be one cool dude." Otherwise, she wouldn't have that huge smile on her face.

"He is."

She's silent after that, and that's how I know she's worn out from the infection. I hold her closer to me.

I shouldn't like how easy it is to want to like Leigh. For her to want to keep touching me. For me to want to tell her all of my goddamn secrets along with my heartaches.

Shoving aside these wants of mine, I make sure I

have a firm grip on her before I grab her housekeys off the coffee table and exchange them with the truck keys in my pocket. Leigh pulls the front door shut after us, and I let us inside my truck.

"Seven, can I ask a favor?"

"Yeah." I buckle her in, and soon, we're barreling down the interstate toward the community hospital in the neighboring town of Delridge.

"If I pass out, don't let them undress me completely. Tell them I'd like to keep my underwear and tank top on."

"They'll want to do a thorough head-to-toe check, Leigh. Make sure you don't have other scratches on your body."

"I'm eighteen, an adult. I have a say in what I show and don't show."

Her defiance is dangerous.

"*Leigh.*"

"Please. Be my advocate."

Leigh begging? I should take advantage and demand she give me something in return for saving her ass, again, but I'm not feeling it.

"Okay, you have my word."

"Thank you."

She reaches over, grasps my hand in hers, and that's when I know I'm in deep shit. The blood is pumping through my heart so fast and hard, I hear the damn beats in my ears.

"One more thing."

"Yeah?"

I glance sidelong at her, not liking how weak she sounds.

"You doing this for me doesn't make us friends. Not now. Not ever."

I can live with that. I don't want to be Leigh's friend either.

I drift in and out of consciousness. Or am I asleep and having a nightmare?

At the moment, I don't care. Seeing my parents again is surreal even if this is a dream or my imagination. *Or a sick joke, baby girl.* The arrogance in *his* tone grates on my nerves.

What right does he have existing in *my* head after I've shut out thoughts of him with his death?

I ball my hands at my sides and glare at the closed bedroom door. He's in my mother's bedroom. Tony's men watch the apartment building and inform him of my dad's comings and goings. It's how Tony has easy access to my mother.

He comes in our apartment building through a back entrance from the alley. I followed him once when I suspected something was going on with my mother.

Around the time my dad left to go work his odd jobs in our crappy, crime-infested neighborhood and sometimes beyond Oakland to San Francisco's Chinatown, my mother would push me out the front door and demand I go learn how to make dumplings with Grandma Chu.

Grandma Chu isn't my real grandma, but I call her that because she spoils me, keeping tamarind candies special in the cupboard for me. There are also flat fortune cookies. Mochi too. It doesn't take much to convince me to run off and visit with Grandma Chu.

After the third time in a week of my mom asking, curiosity got the better of me. I hung back by a dumpster and watched a man slip behind the apartment building using the alleyway in the back.

Unlike my father, who reminds me of a prince with his lean build and air of sophistication, this man looks like one of those fighters the elders watch on television at Grandma Chu's.

He is taller than my dad's five-feet-eleven inches, and has thick arms and a thick neck. Tattoos in bold colors cover his arms while his beard draws my attention to where he doesn't have hair—his head.

On his square face, his nose is crooked. *Broken.* Compared to my dad with his movie star good looks, Tony looks like a criminal and sneaks around like one too.

The stretch of alleyway he uses to get to the back door is dangerous. Drug deals and prostitution happen back there. Only the clueless or the dangerous take that back route to get to the mini mart and liquor store at the other end of the alley.

Tony used my mother's beauty and gentle soul for his own pleasures. Held his position as a police officer over my mother's head. Threatened to destroy my family with his family's wealth. Tony came from old money.

If he ever hears a peep on the streets of him associating with trash like us, he'll get my dad on possession of a firearm. That was the threat he used to keep my mom in her place and what my mom relayed to me to keep me obedient. It's unlawful for a felon to own a gun in the state of California.

I walk up to my parents' bedroom door. My hands clench and unclench. My gaze strays to the glass paperweight on the windowsill. The blue octopus with its tentacles draped over a clear boulder is the prettiest thing in our small one-bedroom apartment.

My parents and I share their queen-size bed. I always knew when they wanted "alone" time. Dad and I would pitch a tent in the living room, and he'd tell me a story of how he and my mom met. His voice is deep and comforting.

I love the sound of his laughter when he gets to the best stories. They're the ones of him and Mom pulling pranks on one another.

One involved cornstarch and food coloring. Imagine my dad's surprise when he pulled a string on a box and it exploded with pink powder. Yes, that was a gender reveal for my dad courtesy of my mom's creative brain. My mother was only nineteen when she gave birth to me. It's crazy to think she was my age when she got knocked up.

Mom pleaded with me to keep what Tony was doing to her a secret from my dad. She demanded my absolute obedience. How could I refuse when she had tears in her eyes? My mom rarely cried. Isn't in the business of begging, either. My father is a criminal. Show weakness around him and he'd take advantage.

That was what Grandfather warned me before he passed away. Aside from my parents, he was my only living relative. Until Dad dropped the news on his deathbed that he wasn't my biological father.

"Find Thomas and Eleanor Stevenson. Threaten him with a paternity suit. He is your real dad, Leigh. Be disobedient and defiant. But always for the right reasons."

And then he was gone, and my world transformed from worse to godawful unbearable.

I tear my gaze away from the paperweight and stand next to the door. There's grunting and the creaking of the bedframe. I squeeze my eyes shut and take deep breaths in and out.

I need to cool my temper and remember that my loyalty firmly belongs with my mother. I don't want my father to go to prison. We don't need Tony's men and his family harassing mine. I'll stick with the status quo for now.

But the minute Tony makes my mother cry again, I'll defy to my heart's content.

Be disobedient and defiant.

But always for the right reasons.

He might not be my father, but I am proud to call Alistair Kim my dad.

8

SEVEN

*O*n the way to the hospital, Leigh goes in and out of consciousness. I step on the gas pedal. The scenery passes by in a blur. Soon, we're at the hospital. I come to a screeching stop in front of the double doors of the emergency department and rush out of the truck.

I sprint around to the passenger-side door, and with Leigh in my arms, I run inside, calling out for help.

The staff come at me with a stretcher. I set Leigh on it and give the nurses the story. "Gash to the back of her right thigh. Might've swallowed bad pool water last night."

They wheel her into a room and pull the curtains closed. Leigh moans, and her eyes flutter open.

"Seven?"

"I'm here." I step around the nurse and lay my hand on Leigh's shoulder.

Worry lines stretch across her forehead. "My clothes—"

"You decide what comes off."

"Sweatpants and sweatshirt only."

The nurses listen and help her out of her clothes. They get Leigh into a gown two sizes too big for her skinny body. One nurse puts an IV in the back of Leigh's hand. Another hooks Leigh to a heart monitor and gets her vital signs.

Other people come into the exam room and ask a bunch of questions. I find out Leigh doesn't have a middle name, she's on birth control pills, and she's allergic to strawberries of all things.

"Leigh, I should step out."

"I'd like for you to stay if you don't mind."

Do I mind? Hell no.

After the nurse draws blood and starts a bag of fluids in her IV, the doctor comes in. He gestures for me to sit. I pull up a chair. Leigh reaches for my hand. I grasp her hand in mine. Her skin is hot, and her grip, weak.

"Miss Kim, I'm Dr. Anderson. The nurse showed me your vital signs. Your blood pressure is low, your heart rate is over one hundred, and you're running a fever of 101.3. They said you have a gash on the back of your leg and that you swallowed pool water. We'll get a chest x-ray. Make sure you don't have pneumonia. May I see your leg?"

Leigh rolls onto her stomach. Streaks of red go up and down her leg.

"When was the last time you ate or had something to drink?"

"Toast for breakfast, but I couldn't keep it down. Same with water."

"Miss Kim, you'll need to be admitted for antibiotics, something for the fever, and hydration."

He instructs the nurse help Leigh onto her back. The nurse lifts the head of Leigh's gurney. The doctor shines a light in her eyes. Asks her to open her mouth. He listens to her heart and her lungs. Zones in on her face.

"May I ask what happened to your temple and your lip?" He shifts his attention to me.

"Seven stays," she says, preempting the doctor's intention of asking me to leave. I get it. He thinks I gave Leigh the injuries.

"I heard a dog whimpering in the middle of the night last night. I thought it was hurt. I went after it, tripped, and hit my face on the tractor."

I cry bullshit.

"And the gash on the back of your leg?"

"The dog ran past and scared me. I backed up and scraped my leg on something metal."

Double bullshit. The doctor looks as skeptical as I'm feeling, but he doesn't question her further.

The door opens, and the curtains part. A guy wheels in one of those portable x-ray machines. The doctor and I step out. He thanks me for bringing her to the ER.

"You saved her life, son. Had you waited any longer, she could've gone into septic shock."

I don't want to minimize how sick Leigh is, but that girl has as many lives as a cat. The x-ray guy backs out of the room. A nurse rushes past me with another bag in her hand. I'm guessing it's Leigh's antibiotic.

"We'll work on getting her a room. I'll check on her again before they take her to the unit."

"Thank you, sir."

I head back inside the room, grab a chair, and bring it to the side of the bed.

"Should I text Hannah? Or Thomas? My dad has his number." In case of an emergency.

"Can we keep this between us?"

"They'd want to know."

"Please, Seven."

Again, she's begging. The bastard in me wants to pounce on her fear, but I don't have it in me to kick her when she's down. What's the fun in that?

"Fine, but this is your one pass. Don't ever beg or ask for a favor again unless you're willing to work for it or give up something in return. Deal?"

She closes her eyes and smiles. "No mercy. I like that. It's a deal. Thanks, Seven, for not making it easy for me."

A girl thanking me for giving her grief?

Doesn't happen, and that's how I know Beautiful Defiance plans on wrecking my world, smashing to smithereens my bastardly heart.

$\mathcal{I}$ stay with her, leaving the room only to use the bathroom and to get something to eat from the cafeteria. The next evening, they discharge her with a week's worth of antibiotics.

The color is back in her face, but she isn't steady on her feet. What's also returned is her defiance. Leigh put up a good fight, not wanting to be taken out in a wheelchair to my truck.

But when she swayed as the nurse helped her dress, she conceded. Thank fuck she cooled her defiance long enough for me to get her ass in my ride.

When we arrived at the Stevenson's place, I opted for the shorter route to Leigh's place. I park my truck alongside the property line, carry her in my arms, and carefully get us over the low-lying fence.

She buries her face in my hair, and every cell in my body comes to attention, same as it did last night. Last night, she'd tossed and turned in her hospital bed. Sometime around two in the morning, she broke her fever. The nurses were kind enough to change out the damp sheets for fresh ones.

While they did, I held Leigh in my arms. Her breathing was rhythmic, a sign to come that she'd fall fast asleep, hopefully more soundly this time. Me, on the other hand, my breathing was shallow and labored. It was sheer torture holding Beautiful Defiance's body close to mine.

I make my way down the hill, careful not to run into the whimpering stray dog, the sharp piece of metal, or the damn tractor. The things that attacked Leigh in her imagination. Yeah, I'm being sarcastic as fuck.

"Doing okay?" It boggles my mind that a man as smart as Thomas would have a guesthouse built at the bottom of two steep hills.

"Yes, thank you."

Before Leigh went to the medical unit, the emergency room doctor delivered the double whammy. Not only did Leigh have a festering infection in her leg, but she had the beginnings of pneumonia from aspirating pool water.

Finally, we're at the front door. I pride myself in not huffing and puffing from carrying her the distance. Not that she's a load of bricks or anything. Leigh is light. Skinny. Needs more meat on her bones.

"Where to? Bedroom? Couch?"

"Bedroom," she says, her voice scratchy.

I walk us inside the bedroom.

"Are you up to eating something?" It's after six.

By the time I ran down to the hospital pharmacy for her medicine, only to wait for Leigh to be done with defying the nurse's suggestion she be wheeled out, her discharge was delayed by two unrelated things.

One, a patient in the next room spiraled downhill and a code was called overhead. Soon after, there was a fuck load of commotion. Fifteen minutes later, a patient across the hall from us went bonkers, and security had to be called.

We stayed in Leigh's room behind closed doors until the yelling stopped and Leigh's nurse returned. Yeah, that was our action for the day.

She holds on to my shirt and rests her head in the crook of my neck. Her hair is soft on my skin, and her puff of warm breath does crazy things to my junk. I mentally tell my excited dick to calm the fuck down. This isn't the time to be at full mast.

"Soup would be nice," she says, bringing my mind back to the topic of getting her fed. "Whatever they have at the Soup Kitchen. I'll pay you back."

"No need. My treat."

"Thanks, Seven." She slips off her shoes and crawls under the covers. "Don't forget the house key."

Good thing she reminded me. I would've forgotten. I leave and lock the door behind me. Inside my truck, I check my messages. There are a shit ton of them from the guys.

Something to the effect of coach benching me if I miss another practice. And why the hell did I miss practice? The team and the school are counting on me to be a leader. Who wants to follow a loser? This from Malice. Screw him.

Leigh being sick is none of their business. But that pneumonia of hers . . . I'm gonna kick Henry's ass the next time he shows his face in Cambridge.

No one messes with a girl to the point she goes in and out of consciousness and has to be admitted to the hospital. Also, whoever fucked up Leigh's face, I'll be looking for that asshole too.

I send the guys a text. "See ya tomorrow, fuckers."

Short. Sweet. No weakness. Top of my game. Their *leader*. I don't wait for a reply. A girl's counting on me to get her food.

I hurry to the Soup Kitchen and order soups and sandwiches. I also stop by the mini-mart and buy pints of ice cream in different flavors in case Leigh's craving sweets.

At her place, I put the ice cream in the freezer, then head inside the bedroom. Moonlight shines in through the parted curtains. Leigh is sleeping facing the wall. The covers are bunched near her waist, and her hair is pulled off to the side and draped over her shoulder. Did her fever return?

So as not to wake her, I skim my fingers down her neck. She'd taken off her sweatshirt, leaving her in her tank top. Her skin is warm but not overly feverish. I stop touching her and inch back. The tattoo at the base of her neck catches my eye.

It's a heart spliced in half by a solid black line, the line extending above and below the heart. I trace the outline of the heart and the intersecting solid line.

"Symbols of my life."

Leigh awake doesn't catch me off guard. The moment I touched her neck, she'd awoken. The nerves on my fingertips were aware of every hitch in her breathing.

"I only see a heart, Leigh."

"Look closer."

I do, and it hits me what they are. "Backward Ds."

"Dismay. Disloyal. Destruction. Disillusioned. I've been and seen all that and more."

"Leigh." I go to stroke her hair, then think better of it.

What she named off is what I don't want in my life. It's best I leave those things to live inside her, to have it inked on her skin, not seen by her eyes, but never to be removed either without it causing her pain.

"Don't feel sorry for me."

"I couldn't care less what you've been or seen." Not true. I don't want to care *too* much.

She rolls onto her back and pushes herself up into a sitting position. She moans and closes her eyes.

"Ugh, too fast."

I plop down next to her on the bed. "You okay to eat?"

"Yes." She leans into me.

"I can bring the food in here."

"The kitchen is fine. Can you stick close by in case I get dizzy?"

"Yeah, sure."

She rises slowly to her feet, waits a few seconds, and then shuffles out of the bedroom and into the kitchen. The hallway isn't wide enough for two people to walk side by side. I hang back with my hands near her waist in case I need to grab her if she decides to keel over and kiss the floor.

At the kitchen table, I rush around her and pull out a chair, being careful not to brush my hulking body on her slight form. It'd be my luck for Leigh to get this far only for me to kill her progress with an accidental body check.

I open the containers of soup and set Leigh's in front of her. "Ask and you shall have."

What the fuck came out of my mouth? I'm a moron. But not a pussy-whipped moron. Huge difference. After I make sure Leigh won't keel over sideways and fall out of her chair, I grab plates from the cupboard and set our sandwiches on them. I put the plate in the center of the table. She tips her head back in the direction of the fridge.

"Help yourself to juice and soda."

"I'm good, thanks."

We eat in silence. While she's occupied with her

soup, I discreetly check out her living space. Small tan couch. White square coffee table. A television mounted on the wall. Tall palm-like plants next to the large windows on either side of the front door.

The place is a decent size for one person, and spotless. Points to Leigh. Good luck finding anything in my room.

"When did you move in?"

"The same week Henry left for DU."

"What happened to his stuff?" I'm assuming this used to be Henry's pad.

"Don't know. The place was empty when I got here."

"Where'd you move from?"

"Why the questions?"

"We're neighbors."

"And here I thought you were trying to be my friend."

"Is that a bad thing?"

"With a guy like you? Yes."

"How'd you figure?"

"A girl can't be just friends with you, Seven. They'll catch feelings and you'll either make them a temporary fascination or you'll keep them firmly in the friend zone. Either way, the girl gets hurt and you get away scotch free. It's the reason I'd rather have you as my enemy. It hurts less that way."

Her eyes widen. She ducks her head and concentrates on scooping up her chicken noodle soup and spooning it into her mouth.

I sit back and slide my arm on the back of the empty chair next to me. *It hurts less that way.* Her words speak to me. Yeah, giving a flying fuck gives someone the power to hurt you. It's the reason I haven't let a girl get close to me.

What else do Leigh and I have in common? I should drop the idea of getting to understand her and her life better. I'm not in her life to make it wonderful and shit. I'm here to make her fall in line and accept the status quo. Before I get in over my head, I stop with the questions and focus on my high maintenance stomach.

Working out every chance I get in the home gym as well as daily practices on the field has upped my body's demand for calories.

After we're done eating, I clean off the table, insisting Leigh sit her ass down when she tried standing and listed off to the side. I caught her before she could hit the floor.

"What's the next step?" I hold her upright with my hands on her shoulders.

"Shower, then bed."

She closes her eyes and blows out a quiet breath. This protective surge crests over me. I pick her up, hold her close, and we make our way inside her bedroom.

We work as a well-oiled team. With her in my arms, I tip her low. She grabs a pair of undies and a camisole from her dresser. I try not to stare at the white undies and peach camisole she has clasped to her chest. The thin camisole won't hide her tits from my greedy eyes. Her white underwear will draw my attention to the patch of dark hair between her legs.

Talking down my hormones, I set Leigh on her feet in front of the bathroom. One of her hands rest on my shoulder, and the other on the spot over my heart.

"Thanks for your help, Seven. Can you lock the door behind you when you leave?"

"I'm not going anywhere. Your couch has my name on it."

There's no defiance on Leigh's part. Or complete acceptance, either. What passes between us is what I call a temporary cease-fire.

"I'll wait outside the door, unless you would rather I come inside?"

I'm not a perv. I honestly don't want her keeling

over and hurting herself. I'll never forgive myself if Leigh gets hurt on my watch.

"Out here is fine," she says. "Thanks."

While she takes her shower, I pace outside the door. Every nerve in my body stands on end, ready to fire the signal to my brain that I need to haul ass inside the bathroom at the hint of Leigh in trouble.

The water shuts off. Metal slides over metal. Then there's silence, followed by the hair dryer. After she shuts off the hair dryer, the toilet flushes then there's running water. She must be brushing her teeth. The door opens and I can't stop staring at the scrape on her face or the cut on her bottom lip. Imperfections, and I'm seething. Whoever marred Beautiful Defiance's face will pay for fucking up what's mine.

Mine?

Yeah, mine to harass and wear down until she worships me like the other girls do.

All thoughts of breaking her of her defiance leave my brain the moment Leigh rests against the wall. She closes her eyes, and her chest rises and falls in this slow ebb and flow of breaths. Is she getting worse instead of better?

"Leigh, can I put my hand on your forehead?"

She nods.

I check her for a fever. She's warm from her shower but not feverish.

"I'm going to pick you up and put you in bed."

I slide my arm under her knees and pick her up. Inside the bedroom, I set her on the bed.

"I'll be right back. You need to take another dose of medicine."

I hurry to the kitchen and grab her bottle of meds and a glass of water. I return to the bedroom, shake out the pills, and hand them and the glass to her. She takes the antibiotics, follows it with a chug of water, and sets the glass on the nightstand.

"You've done so much. How will I ever repay you?"

She licks her lips. I stare at her mouth. Her eyes widen.

"Anything but a kiss. You're underserving of my first kiss, Seven."

A kiss isn't what I'm after. The damn cut on her bottom lip pisses me off to no end. I hate the jerk who dared hurt her. I'm also pissed she won't give me his name.

"You should get some rest. If you need me for anything, anything at all, wake me, you hear?"

"Thanks, Seven."

"Goodnight, Leigh."

"Night."

I get off the bed and walk out of the bedroom with my hands jammed in my pockets, her words looping through my head. *You're underserving of my first kiss.*

I'm underserving? Her first kiss? What she says brands my flesh. It hurts and leaves a lasting mark. I flop onto the couch and stare at the ceiling.

I don't need a kiss from Beautiful Defiance to consider us good and even for me saving her life. Or for her to give me the jerk's name who hurt her. Some way, somehow, I'll find the guy who ruined the perfection of her face.

10

SEVEN

hree years ago ...

"MEISA, YOU'RE A TERRIBLE SWIMMER."

"Am not."

"Are too."

"Go drown a cat, Seven."

"I'm not for cruelty toward animals, so no go. Anyway, is that the best you got?" I raise a brow. The gesture gets all the girls hot for some reason.

"What would you have me say? Go kiss a hairy toad?" She flips her long black hair behind her shoulder.

"Toads aren't hairy. They're just ugly."

"And gross."

"Bloated too," I throw in for good measure. "They're gas balls ready to explode."

She scrunches her face, and I can't stop staring.

Meisa Okamoto, the Japanese exchange student spending the summer with Rue and Riley's family, is pretty. She also has a weird sense of humor, another turn-on for me.

"I'll show you I'm better than terrible."

She takes off her clothes, revealing a swimsuit. Damn her. She lured me to the dock with the promise of a kiss, but intended on doing something else.

"Meisa, what the hell are you doing?"

"Something I should've done the moment I caught you kissing another girl." She balls her clothes and throws the pile at me. "Stop me if you dare, Seven."

She tips her chin and backs up toward the edge of the dock. She's defying *and* daring me to stand by and witness her show of recklessness?

"It's too far to the other side," I growl.

"Dangerous too?"

"Yes." I snatch her clothes off the ground and toss them at her. "Get dressed. We'll do something safe, like archery and mountain biking."

"I don't want safe. You like dangerous, and I want you to like me."

"It doesn't take defiance to do that. I already like you."

She's at the edge of the dock. I look past her shoulders. There's nothing for her to grab on to if she gets tired. There's only open water. I stretch out my hand.

"Come on, Meisa. You know I'm not the greatest swimmer."

"Admit it, you're *terrified* of the water."

I am after I almost drowned. Or should I say, I did drown. That's what my father said.

He yanked me out of the lake and performed CPR after I swung off a rope swing and then passed out when I bore down for the impact. Yeah, it's embarrassing as fuck knowing that the Valsalva maneuver, as the medical professionals called it, killed my showing off to a bunch of girls, and killed me, too, before Dad saved my life.

"I'm not admitting shit. But I will if you get your clothes back on and stop with this defiance crap of yours. The counselors gave us explicit orders to stay away from the water unless they're out here too."

"Following the rules is cowardice and boring."

"If it keeps you alive, then I'd rather you stick with being less reckless and courageous."

"I'm reckless and courageous?" Her face lights up.

"That's not what I mean. You're putting words in my mouth."

"Go eat crow, Seven."

"I will after you drop the idea of ever swimming to the other side of the lake. Promise?"

I'll eat crow. Eat disgusting Brussels sprouts. Eat any goddamn vegetable my mother sets in front of me. I'll do anything to get Meisa's promise.

"No can do. I'll wave to you from the other side."

She launches herself backward and hits the water with a loud splash. I hurry to the edge of the dock. Meisa glides through the water backward. The sun's out, but the lake is surrounded by large and tall trees. The shade drops the temperature of the water to ice cold.

"Meisa, get your ass back here," I call out to her.

She flips me the bird.

Grinding my teeth, I sprint to the boathouse at the other end of the dock. I'm not a great swimmer, but I can float my way to her. I grab a life jacket and strap it on, hurrying back to the edge of the dock. I look for Meisa's dark head of hair. I don't see her.

Where the hell is she? I call out to her again. Nothing.

My scream of terror lodges in my throat. My gut knots. I dive in after her. My fists punch the water. My legs kick in and out. The life jacket keeps me afloat, but the weight of my wet clothes drags me down.

I swim harder and faster until I'm in the middle of the lake. I spin around in circles, searching for a sign of Meisa. Small hands circle my ankles and drag me underwater. Down. Down. Down.

It's pitch black. The hands let go. A face floats in front of me. Wisps of long black hair. Eyes wide open. Lifeless amber eyes. *Meisa.*

"No! No! Don't die on me. Please. No." I clasp her face in my palms. Press my mouth on hers. "Breathe, damn it. Breathe."

Life shines back in her eyes. Her body lights up in this soft glow. She smiles. "Seven. It's okay. I'm okay."

"I'm sorry. I'm so sorry I didn't save you in time."

"You did save me. Thank you, Seven."

She leans in and presses her lips to mine. I close my eyes. This isn't real. Meisa is dead, and nothing, including a different ending to my nightmare, will bring her back to life.

11

I wake up to a weight on my body and a curtain of hair on my face. When the hell did Leigh make her way from the bedroom to the couch? Fuck, did she need something and I was deep in my nightmare?

Doesn't matter. What matters is she's safely in my arms. I swipe aside her hair, and not wanting to wake her, I adjust her body so that she's closer to the back cushions rather than the edge of the couch, and her cheek is resting in the crook of my neck. I'm not stealthy enough.

Her eyes flutter open, and covering her yawn, she locks her gaze on mine.

"What time is it?"

"Good morning to you too."

"*Seven.*"

"Early," I say.

"What day is it?"

"A school day."

"Shit."

"I second that." I slide my arm across her lower back, wanting to stay in this position for as long as possible.

Leigh has other ideas. Of course she does. She peels my arm off her back and rolls off me and onto the floor. She reaches for her cellphone on the coffee table and glances at the screen.

"Five-thirty. I'll make the bus."

"Why when you can climb back on top of me, we can snooze for awhile longer, and I'll drive us to school?"

"Be seen with you? Uh-uh."

She stands, and sliding her fingers in her hair, she shakes out the strands, then combs her fingers through them.

"What's wrong with being seen with me?"

"One, your entourage of girls will come after me, harassing me to no end. Two, Thomas gave me strict orders to stay away from you. Something to do with your dad disliking gold diggers and any girl without pedigree is seen as one. And three, me and you are not friends. We already agreed on that, remember?"

Yeah, I see her points. They're valid except the one about my dad. A girl started that rumor after I didn't return her interest. Girls can be fickle that way.

"Leigh, I saved your life. You owe me."

"Are you *guilt-tripping* me into being your friend?"

"Fuck sakes, no. I'm good with us being frenemies."

"Jesus, how do you know that word? Never mind, we are more enemies than friends."

"Yeah, okay."

"That's not convincing, Seven. Pinky swear."

"I'm not one of your *girlfriends*, Leigh." I rise off the couch and stand.

"No, duh. You have something between your legs they don't have."

I roll my eyes. Jesus H. Christ, I *rolled* my goddamn eyes like I'm an exasperated girl. When I get a chance, I better check and make sure I have a dick. I'm beginning to think being around Leigh is reducing me to being a pansy-ass pussy.

"Pinky swear," she says.

"Negatory that. My word is good."

"Not for me. How about a handshake or a fist bump?"

"Uh-uh. We do something reserved for us."

Her eyes narrow. "What exactly would that be?"

"You kiss the right corner of my mouth, and I kiss your left."

"From what vantage point? Me looking at you? That would make your right my left. Or am I kissing what is your right if I were to stand behind you?"

She smirks.

This girl and her smart-assery.

I throw my hands in the air. "Choose a side, Leigh. How about that?"

"Sure. Less thinking involved."

No shit. I'm already thinking long and hard on what her lips will feel like on my skin.

"Okay, close your eyes, Seven."

I shake my head. Stroke my chin. Tsk for good measure. "Sorry, Defiance, but I have a say in how this goes down, and my say is my eyes stay open. Now if *you* prefer to close yours—"

"Nope."

"We're agreeing?"

"Apparently?" She shrugs.

I smile, liking too much that we're on the same wavelength.

"Do it already so I can give you a chaste-as-fuck peck."

"So eloquent." She steps closer. "So romantic." Crowds my space. "So utterly Seven."

She stands on the tips of her toes, and like a stupid insect caught in the web of the wily spider, I watch her face come closer to mine, my heart ratcheting against my ribcage and my mouth going dry.

Her lips connect with the flesh at the corner of my mouth. I shouldn't be getting off on how soft her lips are on a part of me that doesn't get any action. I prefer a girl's mouth on other parts of my body. But electric heat zings up and down my body and settles in my crotch. A groan slips from me.

Leigh lingers, and another groan starts at my core, travels to my chest, and threatens to edge out from between my clenched jaw. Leigh's lips, soft like cotton, are killing me softly. Not to mention the cut on her bottom lip intensifies the experience, lending a roughness to the softness, and it gets me damn hard.

My fingers itch to grasp her by the waist and yank her against the bulge in my pants. Her lips still on my skin, she raises a brow, daring me to go with the dangerous thought.

We're not doing this to take this situation of ours from frenemies to friend zone to something dumb like boyfriend-girlfriend in two seconds flat. We're doing this because my word isn't good enough for Beautiful Defiance. I'll show her which one of us calls the shots around here.

I step back and swipe my palms on my jeans. Yeah, I'm not turned on by that closed-mouth kiss. Not even a little bit.

"My turn."

"Do you mind if we sit? I'm worn out." Shaky smile from her.

"Aw, shit, your cut and the pneumonia. I'm sorry, Leigh. It was dumb of me to forget."

"If it makes you feel better, I forget stuff when you're around."

That so?

How about I help her forget catching the bus?

She sits on the couch. I grab a spot next to her. Turning into her is awkward. I propose a dangerous idea. A way of punishing her for saying something that strips away another layer of armor over my heart.

"Straddle you?"

"Yeah. Look, I'm not happy about it either, but one kink in my back and I could be out for the season. You don't want everyone mad at you because you kinked my back, do you, Leigh?"

"Seriously?" She narrows her eyes. "God, Seven, you don't ask for much, do you?"

I shrug. "Hey, I want us to be safe."

"Straddling you is the very definition of unsafe." She chews on her bottom lip.

"Scared?" I lean into her.

"No!"

"Then what's the problem, Defiance?"

Tipping her chin at me, she climbs onto my lap and straddles my thighs.

"Happy?"

"Mmm, hell yeah."

"Wipe the grin off your face, Seven."

"I will if you tip my way. Remember, we don't want to kink my back."

She rolls her eyes but leans forward. "You know, I feel sorry for whichever girl makes the mistake of falling for you. You're a pain in the ass."

"Ditto for you."

Another eyeroll from her. I zone in on the corner of her mouth. She's not near enough. I cup the back of her head and bring her closer. She's so close, I see her pupils dilating. Such clear amber eyes. And those full red lips.

"Leigh." My voice is husky, low.

The package in my pants grows. Does she feel me? Fuck yeah, she does. Her eyes widen. Her lips part. Satisfaction courses through me. She's as affected by me as I am by her. I grasp her hips and will her with my mind for her to grind on me. She's wearing her white lace-trimmed undies.

"Are you wet, Leigh?"

"That's none of your business."

Before the school year is through, I plan on making it my business.

"Do it already, Seven. I have a bus to catch."

I would, but I like this slow burn between us.

"You should've taken me for my word. We wouldn't be in this *precarious* position."

"Such a big word from the jock who's failing two of his classes."

"How—"

"I have my ways."

"Do tell?"

"Why do you need to know?"

"I'd like to punch the face of the person who told you, that's why. Failing anything is embarrassing as fuck."

"No one snitched on you. When I went looking

for your locker combo, I might've 'stumbled' onto your grades."

She air-quoted "stumbled." Stumbled my ass. She went looking for something to hold over my head in case she couldn't, one, steal the battery from my truck and two, booby trap my locker. Leigh is a piece of work, and the way her mind works is turning me the fuck on.

"You are ruthless."

"How so?"

I call her out.

Her amber eyes sparkle. "Caught. Will ruthless be your next nickname for me?"

"Hell no, I won't give you the satisfaction."

"Darn."

Small smile from her, and damn it, she is beautiful.

I shift my pelvis upward the same time she rolls her hips. Her heat cocoons my dick. I groan.

"Leigh, *fuck*."

"Sorry, *big guy*, but we're not going there."

My big guy twitches in my pants. I groan, again. "Brutal. You. Are. Brutal."

She laughs. "Next move is yours to make."

I dig my fingers into her skin. Open my mouth.

She shakes her head. "Keep to the kiss. Chaste. No tongue action."

Damn, and here I thought I could tongue that sinful corner. I move my hands from her hips to the sides of her face. My eyes open, I press my mouth on the corner of hers. Her skin is soft. Warm. Smooth. I inhale. Flowers and vanilla. Sweet. I could eat her up. Eat her out. Bury my nose in the curve of her neck. Bury my face against her pussy. She'd be wet on my face. Sweet on my tongue.

That's what I imagine Leigh would be like and taste like. I've never gone down on a girl, but for Leigh to feel all sorts of good, I'll do it.

Except Leigh's not a casual hookup type of girl. She's after a relationship, and I'm not looking for a girlfriend. Casual is all I'll offer a girl. I drop my palms from her face and sink back into the couch.

"Get cleaned up. Get something in your stomach for your meds."

She gets up off my lap. Thank fuck. I was seriously rethinking the casual-relationship thing during my speech.

Leigh stands. Sways. I lurch up and clasp on to her waist. "Hey, there. No need to hurry. We have more than enough time."

"I'm not riding in with you."

"I saved your life. You owe me. Owing me is getting a ride from me. Easy as pie."

"Easy isn't what I need. We agreed on that."

"You're sick."

"I'm better."

She puts her hands on my chest and pushes. I don't budge.

"Leigh."

"Don't, Seven. I don't need your pity or your mercy."

"Then I won't give it, but it doesn't take away the obvious. You owe me for saving your life."

Hard glint in her amber eyes. Locking of her jaw.

"Like I've said before, I'm not in the business of owing anyone anything."

She marches to her bedroom and returns with a black plastic bag in her hands.

"Here's your helmet and your pads. You'll need them for practice."

"What the hell?" I snatch the bag from her. "When did you steal these?"

"The night you saved me from Henry."

"While I was *sleeping*?" She could've throttled me in my most vulnerable state.

"You weren't home yet. I think you were at that

party being paraded in front of by girls in barely there bikinis."

My irritation drops a notch at what I'm hearing in her voice.

"Are you jealous?" A grin spans my face. Fuck's sake, why does the idea give me a stiffy?

"Why would I be? We're enemies."

"Or we're those kids who pick on one another at recess because we want to play tongue hockey."

"As if."

I drop the bag and cross my arms. "That's immature, Leigh."

"And saying things like tongue hockey isn't?"

"What would you rather I say?"

"Something more mature."

"Like swapping spit? Eat your face? French kissing?"

"That's worse."

"Or how about eating you out? Or making you come on my face? Or wetting my dick pounding inside your snatch bareback."

"Now you're being annoying and crass."

"Should I be immature? Or annoying and crass?"

"How about you and your friends show the girls respect?"

"I will when they start respecting their bodies. Otherwise, it'll be business as usual."

"You're a jerk."

"You're a pain in my ass."

"Good."

"Fine. Have it your way."

"I will. My way suits me."

"Whatever, Misery."

"That's Safari to you, Mister Stick-Up-My-Ass."

"Who's the immature one now?"

She points at the front door. "Get out, Seven. You saved my life. I returned what I borrowed. We're even."

I grab my stuff and stomp out of her place.

Even?

Not by a long shot.

12

*a*s soon as I step inside my first class, I'm told the principal wants to speak with me.

To my surprise and annoyance, Seven is sitting across from the principal. I grab the seat next to him.

"Good morning, Leigh. How are you today?"

He dips his head and glances at me over the rims of his glasses.

"Fine." I wait for him to say his piece. He clears his throat a few times before he does.

"Leigh, it's come to my attention that you have quite the rap sheet. Something that wasn't brought up when your guardian enrolled you in our school."

I sit tall and don't chance a glance at Seven. It's bad enough that the principal is bringing up my past offenses in front of my enemy. Shitty enough, too, that Thomas lied to me.

He said he told the principal about my troubles with the law, including my brief time in juvenile detention. He lied to me *and* Principal Staudinger. Now I have to cover for him and figure out who gave me up. My guess is either Hannah or Henry. Those two hate my guts.

"I haven't let it affect my schoolwork. I'm getting straight A's."

"And you should be proud of turning your life around. I called you to the office to ask for your help."

He wants my help? I should be flattered, but I'm more suspicious than anything. I mean, there's a reason Seven is sitting next to me.

"What would that be?" I ask.

"Seven's grades are suffering, and if he doesn't improve soon, I'll have to ask the coach to bench him. He also missed two practices."

"That's my fault. I was sick, and Seven stayed with me while I was in the hospital."

He looks from me to Seven with disbelief. Seven's partying and those fights of his on and off the field isn't helping his cause.

"It doesn't change the fact I'll have to keep him out of the game tomorrow and possibly next Friday."

"Are you asking that I tutor him?" I cut to the chase. I'm missing math class, and math isn't my strong suit, contrary to the belief that Asians excel in math.

"Yes, that's the point I'm trying to make. I heard you two are neighbors. Leigh, why don't you stick around for Seven's practice? Make sure he shows up. He can give you a ride home afterward, and you two can get studying time in. How about it?"

This can go one of two ways.

I refuse and the entire school somehow finds out and I'll never live it down, certain I'll be harassed until graduation and even beyond. I accept and will still get harassed by the girls for taking up Seven's time.

I begrudgingly accept. No matter whether I swing for refusing or accepting, there is one common goal—Cambridge High winning the championship with its king at the helm.

"Good. You can start next week."

The principal dismisses us. I hurry to class, barely glancing at Ginger, the pretty and quiet blonde from my pottery class, as she looks from me to Seven keeping up alongside me. He's not in a hurry because he's worried he'll miss something important. He's matching my speed-walk, our fingers grazing, because he has something to say to me.

"I don't like this any more than you do."

"Not my fault you partied too hard and now you're failing your classes."

"Do you want us to lose the championship? Hand the win over to the bastards of Delridge?"

"I didn't grow up here, so I couldn't give a care, Seven."

"Wrong. You see, I think you care too much. Want to be a part of something bigger than yourself. Admit it, Defiance."

"So we're back to that, huh?"

"Enemies, remember?"

"Then you should know I won't admit a damn thing to you, Seven Shanahan." God, he is so infuriating.

"Leigh, you care for another reason. You'll hang around for the year and then go to DU like the rest of us. You'll be seeing us on campus."

"I'd rather gouge my eyes out with a plastic spoon than be on the same campus as Henry."

We're nearing math class. Before we get to the door, Seven steers me into an empty hallway and crowds me against the lockers with his arms alongside my head.

"You help me get my grades up, and I'll kick any guy's ass who dares hurt you."

"I'm not doing this for you. I'm doing it for me. I don't want to be the girl known for giving the win to Delridge because I kept the king of the game from playing."

I shove my palms into his chest to get him to move out of my personal space. He doesn't budge. It's like the wind pushing a brick building. Immovable. Impossible.

"And this ass-kicking I'm willing to do for you?"

"I don't negotiate with bullies and guys who have zero respect for a girl's right to sass and defy."

"Why resort to that? Why can't you just be?"

"Follow the crowd?"

"No, Leigh. Accept things as they are."

"Would you give up control and power over the game and the girls?"

"It's not in me to follow. I like being at the top of my game."

"Then don't expect me to change, either, Seven."

I don't have to push him away. He steps aside and lets me go. I rush to class, his intense stare boring into my back. I hold my head high, unwilling to show weakness.

I can never forget who sits at the top of the food chain and that the hunter and the prey aren't meant to cohabit as friends. They will always be foes. That's how the laws of nature work. Survival of the strongest while the weak get stomped on, then eaten alive.

13

*T*he next day, in gym class, I eye the corner where Seven and his ex-girlfriend Allison disappeared to, curious as to whether the two will get back together.

Hannah and her friends went on and on about how Seven hasn't had a serious relationship since his ex-girlfriend cheated on him with a football player from Delridge High their junior year.

That's the ultimate betrayal for someone like Seven, but maybe he's willing to overlook Allison's lapse in judgement and forgive and forget. From my spot by the bleachers, it's obvious Allison was crying. Seven pulled her to him, then led her away from our curious stares.

If they are getting back together, good for him

for giving her a second chance, though the thought doesn't sit well with me. Thankfully, my better side wins out over the vindictive, jealous Leigh Kim.

I shouldn't be a softie toward a cheater, but had Thomas not cheated on his wife, I wouldn't be here. So, I'm willing to give someone a second chance to learn from their mistake. Thomas lying to Principal Staudinger should be strike two against him, but I can understand his point of view for keeping my rap sheet under wraps.

Seven returns to the gym, and the guys are back on for their game of hoops. The girls are sitting on the bleachers, watching them.

We have a substitute teacher for PE, and she's awe-struck by Seven and his friends, giving them a free pass to do whatever they want for the last period of the day. That earned her points from the girls. They shelled out dating advice and makeup tips.

I'd rolled my eyes. Even the teachers are under the reigning king's spell.

Seven grabs a basketball off the floor, and pushing off the toes of his shoes, he shoots. His shirt rides up and shows skin. The girls stare and point at his six-pack abs. Fan their faces, too, when his shorts slide down his hips.

These girls and their out-of-control hormones. Proud of myself for being immune to the king's charms and rock-hard body, I pick up a ball and toss it, knocking his ball away from making the second shot through the hoop.

He glares. "You have a problem with me or something, Safari?"

I smile, happy to be hating on one another again.

"Or something, *Nobody*." I smack my gum. Twirl pieces of hair between my fingers.

Collective gasps echo in the gym that's suddenly gone quiet.

"How about a game of PIG?" I ask. "Or HORSE? Up to you which animal of preference I kick your ass in."

More gasps from the girls. The guys look me up and down and snicker.

"PIG, and we up the ante with a bet."

The girls get off the bleachers and crowd us. They're interested to find out what Seven will do to me should I lose.

"Fine, but the bet stays between us."

Hannah whines. "Not fair."

"It's not up to you," I tell her. "Unless Nobody is too chicken-shit and needs witnesses."

"Pfft. As if."

I hold back my smile.

"Come here." I crook my finger.

Seven heads my way. The sea of girls part. I step up to Seven and am so close, I catch a whiff of male and sweat.

Leaning in, I say near his ear, "If I win, you teach me to drive. If I lose, you get back the lucky coin I 'borrowed' from your pants pocket."

He lurches back. "What the fuck, Leigh?"

Hannah sets her hands on her hips. "What did she say? I have a right to know, Seven. She's staying with my family, and if they're in danger because of her, I'll have to tell my dad and Henry."

"You'll tell them jack shit," he growls. "Leigh's right. This is between me and her." He steps forward and says in a low voice, "You win this time, but next bet, I decide what's at stake."

"Are you speaking of the skin off my back if I lose? Or how about my firstborn? Or is it my defiant soul you're after?"

He chuckles under his breath. The other students and the substitute teacher lean in like they're the Tower of Pisa.

"You're weird."

"Get used to it," I say. "And don't you dare make

Weird into another nickname. Stick with Safari or Defiance, okay?"

"Yeah, I got it."

"Hey, I thought you were sitting out tonight's game?" I say in a quiet voice.

As far as I'm concerned, few people are aware of Seven's failing grades and him getting benched.

"I overheard the girls talking in the bathroom. You're playing?"

The girls spoke excitedly about how they couldn't wait to watch Seven play. He's so hot in his uniform.

"Coach and Principal Staudinger gave me a free pass. My *only* pass."

"Ah, gotcha." Wait a minute, this easy back and forth is too easy. I step back and say for everyone to hear, "Rock, paper, scissors, winner goes first?"

He nods. We chant, "Rock, paper, scissors, shoot." His scissors cut my paper. Darn.

The other students and the substitute teacher line up against the wall. There are fifteen minutes before class ends. We'll need to make this quick; otherwise, I'll miss my bus.

Seven makes the first shot and waits for me to take his spot along the sideline before he hands me the ball. The point of the game is to make the shot from wherever the opponent made the shot.

If I miss the hoop, I earn the first letter. Whoever spells PIG first loses. I overshoot the hoop. Shooting from the sideline is my weak point, and Seven homes in on that.

The rest of his shots are done from the sidelines, resulting in the demise of my pride and the end to our game. The final bell rings, and everyone rushes out of the gym. Seven's friends smack him on the shoulders.

Ginger somehow slips in between Seven and his friends and loops her arm through his, leaning into him and looking up at him adoringly. I want to puke in my mouth. Seven doesn't spare me a backward glance. Instead, he does what he's good at—being a jerk.

"See you later, Safari. Remember to stick with what you owe me."

"If I don't?"

"For real? I know where you live, Captain Underpants."

Does he have a clue there's a cartoon character by that name?

Nonetheless, his comment irks me. Just because I was wearing undies with Captain America's face on my ass the night he took me to the emergency room doesn't give Seven the right to make my crush on Chris Evans fair game.

I do something immature. I stick my tongue out at his disappearing back, then utter words I regret saying as soon as they leave my defiant mouth.

"Next time you stay over, put a sock on the snoring, Seven!"

14

The bus ride home is unbearable. There are pointed glares my way and whispering and snickering. Word travels fast where Seven is concerned. I thought of backtracking and taking back my words, but that's not me.

He did stay the night.

He does snore.

End of story.

The other kids can do with it what they like.

Shoving aside the crappy ending to my day, I get off the bus. Except I'm not ready to go home. Home. Is it, though? A home has a family. My parents are dead. My half-siblings don't know I exist. Same goes for Eleanor.

Sighing, I heft my backpack higher over my

shoulder and turn the other direction toward school. There's a mom-and-pop diner that has to-die-for burgers and milkshakes. I can get two milkshakes to go and if I hurry, Sorrow can enjoy the yumminess before hers turns to mush. Hopefully, her father is out cold. That man is a jumpy drunk.

I touch the faded scrape on my forehead and the healing cut on my bottom lip. It wasn't his fault I surprised him in the darkness, and he shoved me against the brick fireplace, believing I was a burglar.

Technically I am one.

I stole Seven's stuff from inside his bedroom while he was sleeping. Took the lucky coin that dropped from his pants pocket when I moved his pants to get to his football helmet and shoulder pads.

I walk alongside the road and stare straight ahead. Cambridge is a small town, and there's little traffic. But ever since I was almost run over walking home from the school I went to in Oakland, I stay alert to my surroundings. The great thing about game day Friday is the roads are even less busy at this time of day. The other kids are readying themselves for the football game and the after-game parties.

Inside the diner, I set my backpack on the floor

and put in an order for two milkshakes, a chocolate one and a vanilla one.

"Is there a chance there are strawberry bits in the shakes? I'm highly allergic." I nudge my backpack with my sneaker. Inside the inner pocket is my EpiPen.

I went to a place that didn't rinse out the blender well, leaving bits of strawberries stuck on the glass. As soon as I took a bite of my chocolate milkshake, I knew there were strawberries. My tongue tingled, then swelled up. It took weeks for my dad to work off the bill for the ambulance ride and the ER visit.

"There could be. I can use a never-used blender and label it with your name."

"You'd do that?"

"Heck yeah. Anything to keep customers safe."

"Wow, thank you."

He rings me up. I hand him my debit card. He looks at it before running it through the machine.

"Leigh. I like your name. It's different."

He pronounces my name wrong, and I politely correct him.

"It's Leigh, like Bruce Lee."

"Crap. I butchered it. Makes sense, though. You look more like a Lee than a lay."

My eyes must be wide. His sure are.

"Shit. I mean, crap. That came out wrong."

Completely.

He looks so mortified, I stretch out my hand. "Nice to meet you . . ."

I wait for him to give me his name. He's not wearing a name tag.

"Miles. It's Miles."

"I haven't seen you at Cambridge High."

"Don't go there. Graduated last year. My dad wanted me to get my ass to DU, but I can wait a year or two. He needs my help with the diner."

Nice of him. "Do you have openings?"

"If you're up for working every Friday and Saturday night, then yeah, my family can use the help. Game nights are always busy, and Saturdays just are. Does that work?"

"Absolutely. When do I start?"

"Is tomorrow okay? We have tonight covered for Cambridge's home game against Delridge."

A game I won't be at. My dad loved football. When he wasn't working, we would spend Saturdays watching college football and Sundays and Thursdays watching NFL football. That was our dad and daughter routine. To watch football without him... I sigh. I miss him.

"Tomorrow is great. Thank you. I appreciate you giving me a job. I mean, you don't even know me."

"We can talk more. Are you in a hurry? If you are, I can make the shakes so you can get going."

Miles is nice. Easy on the eyes too. He's lanky and tall. Was probably an athlete. I'm guessing track or basketball. His blond hair is short on the sides and unruly on the top. And there is so much depth to his green eyes, a girl can stare into them and lose herself. Miles is gorgeous.

"I'd love to stick around, but my friend is waiting for me."

Sorrow isn't, but I haven't seen her since Seven took me to the hospital, and I need to make sure she's okay. She's not a fan of surprises. Buttering her up with a milkshake will make her less pissed at me for stopping by during daylight hours.

"Is this friend of yours a boyfriend?"

I picture Seven and how his eyes never left mine when we kissed. On the corners of our mouths. God, that was hot. Chaste and simple but so freaking hot.

"Not that you and I should start anything if we're to work together."

Am I dreaming? This guy has the moral compass of an entity.

"A friend girl," I offer. "She's had a rough week. A surprise milkshake will make her day."

"We all need friends, don't we?"

"We sure do."

We smile. He makes the milkshakes. I leave the diner with a spring to my steps. Two friends. I've made two friends, and they are good people. I cannot wait to tell Sorrow about Miles. They would like one another. If only I can get Sorrow to leave her house.

A knocking on my bedroom window startles me. I stop reading the text from Grandma Chu's granddaughter. Who or what is outside my window? It's midnight.

I listen again. Every nerve in my body stands on alert. Silence. I exhale the breath I didn't realize I was holding and go back to reading the text from Rose. I text her, "Sending money now," and keep my word, using Venmo. I hit the side button, ready to turn over for the night. But I hear it again.

Tap, tap, tap. What the hell? I hold the cellphone to my chest and slide farther under the covers. Hannah is at a party. Eleanor and Thomas won't be back from their trip for another week. The only member of the family not accounted for is Henry. Did he return to scare the hell out of me?

I hold still, close my eyes, and listen. *Tap, tap, tap.* Crap! I should call 911. Except I've had mixed experiences with cops and will have to be on my deathbed or someone needs serious help before I'll call them.

My heart beating fast, I get out of bed, and crouched on the floor with my phone in my hand, I crawl on my hands and knees to the window, hold up my phone, and snap a picture.

The flash is bright. The cursing is loud. The person's voice is familiar. I pop my head up and yank open the curtains. Seven is outside with his pretty face pressed up against my window.

Under the moonlight, his hair is damp, and he is wearing a dark hoodie. He looks at me with this intensity in his pool of ink eyes, and goodness, Seven Shanahan is *gorgeous*. Angular face. Full lips. My heart beating faster, I push the window up an inch.

"Why are you here, Seven? Shouldn't you be out partying?"

I didn't ask if Mayhem won over Delridge's football team, the Daredevils.

"I'm here to keep an eye on you. Want to make

sure you don't steal more of my stuff. Let me in, Leigh." He taps on the glass.

"Use the front door."

"Did you?"

"Did I what?"

"Come inside my house through the damn front door?"

"Of course not. I climbed up the tree by your window."

"Point made. Let me in."

In our crouched positions, we are eye to eye.

"Say the magic word." My mouth suddenly dry, I lick my lips. He follows the movement. Seven takes his time responding.

"Please," he finally says, tearing his gaze away from my mouth, looking me in the eyes again.

I take off the screen and open the window as far as it'll go. After he climbs inside, I close the window and leave the screen leaning against the wall. I have a feeling he'll leave the same way he came in. Crazy boy.

He takes off his sneakers and sets them next to the window screen. Then he strips.

"What are you doing?" I rush forward and stop him with my hands on his wrists.

"You said to put a sock on the snoring. I only

snore when I'm uncomfortable as fuck. Three things do that. One, I'm sleeping on someone's lumpy couch. Two, I doze off wearing clothes to bed. And three, I'm *exhausted*."

He was all that on the night he stayed over.

"So, you'll put a sock on it by—"

"Sleeping in my boxers only and sharing your bed, but I am not exhausted. I'm wired, and you're the reason."

"How is it my fault you're inside *my* bedroom at the ungodly hour of *midnight?*"

I let go of his wrists and slip under the covers. Seven strips. I stare at the ceiling. The covers are pulled down. The side of the bed next to me dips. Seven is naked except for his boxers. And he just crawled into my bed. Great.

I scoot as close to the wall as I can without looking like a girl version of Spider Man hanging off the wall sideways. Seven scoots after me. His leg brushes against mine. The hair tickles my sensitive skin, and I bite down on my moan, remembering that only yesterday, I straddled him and almost started grinding on his erection when we kissed.

"Seven, you should stay on your side."

"Why?"

Does he not feel the heat wafting between us?

With me in my skimpy camisole and a pair of lace-trimmed black undies, us in bed like this can get dangerous and dirty real fast.

"It's hot."

"But I'm cold."

"Seven Shanahan, are you *whining?*"

"Yeah."

There's the hint of a smile in his voice.

I blow out an exaggerated sigh. "Fine, but after you get warm, leave breathing room."

"Gotcha. Okay."

He plasters against me. I hold still, not wanting to encourage him to touch me or *something.*

"Back to my question. Why are you wired?"

"We lost the game to those bastards."

"That's my fault how?"

"You have my lucky coin."

His fingertips graze mine. I bring my arm up and rest it on my stomach. Anything to keep us from touching. If I let him touch me, I'll want him to do other things, like kiss me full on the mouth.

"I'm sorry, Seven. I should've brought it to you before the game started." Then I say words that blur the lines. "How can I make it up to you?"

I'm expecting his ask to be dirty. Or for him to

take our corner kisses to the full mouth-on-mouth deal. What he asks for, though, is . . . surprising.

"I'd like to know more about you. Where you grew up. What kinds of parents raised you. What your favorite food is. What your dreams are. Heartaches too. And I'd like to know what parts of Cambridge you'd like to explore."

"Seven Shanahan, are you wanting to spend time with me?" I shift onto my side, and balanced on my elbow, I study his profile.

I left the curtains parted, not trusting myself around Seven in complete darkness.

"Yeah, if it means we can fight so we can kiss and make up afterward."

Sly grin from Seven.

Smiling, I get on my back again and tell Seven of my life. It's so nice to have someone to talk to, and without meaning to, I overshared.

"I grew up in Oakland, California. My mother, Constance Tan, married my father, Alistair Kim, after she had me. She was nineteen, and my father, twenty-five. They died when I was thirteen."

"Aw, I'm sorry, Leigh."

He reaches for my hand under the covers and interlaces our fingers. His palm is rough, and his fingers, big. I concentrate on a spot on the ceiling, my heart beating fast like hummingbird wings.

"What were they like? I mean, aside from the bouts of defiance, you're cool."

A compliment from Seven? I ignore the fast beats of my heart and talk to my heart's desire about the two people I love and miss so much in this world.

"My mother was funny, beautiful, kind, and soft-spoken. She was a seamstress. My father worked odd jobs. They were a good pairing. He was the firecracker to her gentle breeze. Anytime he walked into a room, his presence lit the place up with this contagious energy. If I could bottle it, his energy would have powered an entire block of buildings."

"He was charismatic."

"Yes," I say, in awe of how well Seven understands who my father was.

"I bet he was charming too."

"Very." I bite down on my smile. Seven is charismatic *and* a charmer. The reason his teammates follow his lead and the girls clamor for his attention.

"Did you live with relatives after their deaths?"

"I wish. I spent my years up until a month ago in the foster care system. I turned eighteen on the flight over here. Thomas met me at the airport."

"Are you saying you celebrated a monumental birthday mid-air?"

"No celebrating," I admit.

"That's shitty. I'm sorry, Leigh."

"Not your fault."

"Happy belated birthday."

I wait two beats before answering. After my parents' deaths, no one took the time to wish me a happy birthday.

"Thank you, Seven." I squeeze his hand. He squeezes back. He understands how much his wish meant to me.

"My favorite food is Vietnamese pho," I continue, answering his questions one by one. "No matter sunshine or rain, the soup gives me comfort and reminds me of my parents. My dad worked for this noodle house in Chinatown in San Francisco. They paid him under the table *and* our meals were half off. We didn't go often. Traffic in the area is bad, and my father would rather my mom and I stick close to our apartment building."

"There's a pho restaurant in the town center."

"Really?"

He laughs at the excitement in my voice. "You betcha."

"I'll have to give it a try."

"And your dreams? No need telling me of your heartaches, Leigh. I can already guess what that is."

The tenderness in his voice . . . My throat tightens, and I swallow past the lump lodged there.

Why is he being so nice? Is he tired of me having the upper hand?

Getting outwitted by a girl, a nobody, has got to be an ego-buster for a cocky guy like Seven.

"I would love to work in a large city like Alexandria or Montgomery." I tell him of my dream, starting with where I'd move to.

Alexandria and Montgomery are two large cities north and south of the small college town of Dumas.

"I'd help disadvantaged kids. Show them what resources are out there. Be a mentor. Someone they trust."

"So something along the lines of a counselor?"

"Yes."

"You'd be good, Leigh."

"Except for my rap sheet."

"That was my next question." He lets go of my hand and gets on his side. I do too. We stare at one another. "You don't need to tell if you don't want to. It wasn't a part of my ask, so no biggie."

The thing is, I do. This part of my life I can't tell Sorrow. She has enough troubles on her shoulders.

"Petty theft. Breaking and entering. Grand theft auto. All misdemeanors."

His eyes widen. "No wonder you were able to get in and out of my room without me knowing. You're an *expert*."

Not the expert my dad was until he got caught stealing an EpiPen from the pharmacy. It's the reason he went to prison for two years. Breaking and entering and robbing a business is a felony.

"I also assaulted someone with a bat, Seven. It's the reason I spent time in juvie."

He tucks pieces of my hair behind my ear. "You must've had a good reason."

"I did." I'm ready to get this off my chest. "One of my foster brothers tried raping this girl he lured into an alley. I found an aluminum bat in the dumpster and broke his arm with it, then went for his legs. He swore never to hurt someone again and promised he wouldn't tell a soul."

"You are one hell of a badass, Leigh Kim. But how'd you get nailed with an assault charge if he didn't snitch?"

"The girl did."

"*Fuck*. Again, I'm sorry."

"I'd do it again."

"I'm sure you would. That's who you are."

"Can you see why I can't just be? My dad had charisma and charm. My energy is different. I want to do. To challenge. Otherwise, I get antsy."

"There are other ways to expend that kind of wired energy."

"Like what?"

His gaze drops to my mouth. "Foreplay."

I swat his shoulder, the heat between my legs growing unbearable. Goodness, the intense way he's looking at my lips and licking his, like he wants a mouthful of me . . . "And the prey comes out to play. A wolf in sheep's clothing. I'm not going there with you." I move onto my back and sling my arm over my eyes. "I'll come up with my own methods."

"Like learning to drive? Grand theft auto. Fuck's sake, Leigh, how old were you?"

"Legal. Sixteen." I remove my arm from my eyes and stare at the ceiling. "But I never had formal driver's ed. My foster parents weren't willing to let me learn. It was their way of keeping me out of trouble."

"Yet, you stole a car and took it for a joyride."

"On a dare. If I did so, my foster brother would leave me alone and not come into my room at night."

"You mean he came after you first?" He throws

off the covers and sits up. "Do you have a last known address for this fucker? I'd like to fuck him up."

"Language, Seven." I reach out and pat his shoulder. He does something utterly swoon-worthy. He takes my hand and drops a kiss on my palm.

"The address, Leigh."

"I don't have it. He grew out of the foster system."

"How many homes?"

"Seven over five years. Only one family was decent to me, but they decided not to foster anymore when their daughter became pregnant with twins."

"Shit."

"*Seven.*"

"Crap."

"Better, thank you."

"Back to the foreplay."

"Back to the driving."

We spoke at the same time. He smiles. I do too. The thick tension in the room fades.

"You first," I say.

"I'll table the foreplay for now, but one of these days, I'll save your life again, and that's what I'll be asking for—a taste of you."

Seven's mouth on mine? His tongue circling my nipples? His dark head of hair between my legs? I haven't been properly kissed on the mouth, but I'm not clueless or a prude. I watch porn. I touch myself. To have someone . . . No, not "someone," but to have Seven touch and taste me . . . My panties dampen. I bite down on the moan lodged in my throat.

It's a bad idea, having these sinful thoughts. And the mental images . . . The temptation to offer my body to him is as close as on the tip of my tongue, the word "yes" like an aphrodisiac. I slide away from his sculpted shoulders, the patch of chest hair, and the sinful strip of hair disappearing below the waistband of his boxers. He must be feeling my heat too. He scoots closer to the edge of the bed and slides back under the covers.

"The driving, Leigh?"

"Not your problem. I'll figure it out. It's not like I have a car, though jacking Malice's GT-R would get him indebted to me."

"You *will not* steal his baby. And you won't ever get in a situation where you owe him, Leigh. When a Sterling digs their claws in you and claim you as theirs, you're done for. Them Sterlings are a possessive, jealous bunch. Promise me?"

"I've dealt with guys worse than him. Case in point, there's you."

"Ha-ha. Not. Promise, Leigh?"

"Fine."

"Pinky swear."

"Seven."

"Come on, give it to Daddy, right here."

He gets all up in my personal space and points at the corner of his mouth.

"I will, but don't refer to yourself as 'Daddy' or ever make me call you that."

"Too pervy?"

"God, yes."

He laughs. I drop a quick kiss on the corner of his mouth. He lingers on mine, his arm curving over my hip in this possessive but gentle way.

"Seven, we should call it a night. Or more like morning. I'm working tomorrow."

"Where at?"

"I start my new job at Queenie's Diner."

"You working for Miles Sinclair's family?"

"Yes. Miles is nice. Made sure to give me my own blender so strawberry chunks don't get into it and I go into anaphylactic shock."

"Your allergy is that bad?"

"Packing double EpiPen bad."

"Holy fuck."

"Sucks, really. I used to eat them all the time as a kid, then one day, poof, swollen tongue, eyes, face. It was horrible. I looked like I was stung by a hive of bees on steroids."

"Is there a different fruit you like that makes up for missing out on cha-bies?"

I laugh. "Cha-bies?"

"You like?"

"Sure." I'm too happy to tell him that he sounds juvenile when he says strawberries like he's a little kid. "My other favorite fruit is blueberries. The fatter the better."

"Yum."

"Yep, yum," I agree.

We laugh. I settle further inside the covers, ready for bed. Seven has other ideas. He points to a remote on the nightstand. "What's that?"

"No clue."

"Oh, I think you do. How about I put my guess to the test?"

"*Seven.*"

He turns his back to me and reaches for the remote. I tackle him, but too late, he hits the "on" button. The panel on the ceiling above us opens, exposing the hidden skylight. The moon is hiding behind the clouds again. The stars twinkle at us. It's beautiful, and I hate it.

I face the wall.

"Leigh." A large warm hand settles on my shoulder. Thick fingers sweep aside my hair. He traces the tattoo at the base of my neck. "What's wrong? Why don't you want to stare at the night sky? Hear raindrops on the pane?"

"Too extravagant. I don't want to get used to it. Thomas's world. I don't belong in it."

"Leigh, in this, can you just be and enjoy what you have in the here and now?"

I sigh. How did this boy get to be so wise? Undone by the tenderness in his voice, I scoot close and lay my head on his shoulder. We stare up at the night sky.

"It's breathtaking."

He kisses the top of my head. "I agree. Goodnight, Leigh."

"Night, Seven. Remember, we are not friends."

"Never that, Leigh. Never just friends."

What's he mean by "never just friends?" I don't think too hard on it. My eyelids droop, and I give in to sleep, excited for my first day at my new job.

I wake up to an empty bed. Wondering if last night was a dream, I throw off the covers, sit, and stretch my arms high and tip my face up.

Daylight shines in through the skylight. Seven in my bed wasn't a dream. Smiling, I dress and hurry out of the guesthouse to catch the shuttle into the heart of Cambridge, the town center.

Snagging the job at Queenie's is great, but I'll need more hours to pay off the hospital bill that will arrive soon in the mail. No way will I let Thomas pay for my mistakes even though it was his son who tried drowning me, giving me a case of pneumonia.

Speaking of pneumonia, I take a deep breath. My

lungs aren't tight. The back of my leg doesn't hurt as badly either.

At the end of the road to the Stevenson's mansion, I wait at the shuttle stop. Thank goodness I don't have to wait long. It starts raining. I hop onto the shuttle and tap my pass on the reader next to the driver. There are two other passengers, a woman and her child.

The woman looks to be a few years older than me. Her little boy is sitting on her lap. When the woman notices me staring, she smiles. Friendly. Trusting.

Her reaction is different from what I'm used to. On the city buses, people don't dare make eye contact. It can be misconstrued as challenging or disrespecting someone. I meet her gaze, and smiling back, I grab a seat next to the window.

The ride into the town center is about fifteen minutes, putting us close to the neighboring town of Delridge. Delridge High is Cambridge's rival. I hear their quarterback hates Seven. If both guys decide on attending Dumas University, they'll be fighting for the top spot of starting quarterback.

Tired of the silence and miffed that Seven isn't far from my thoughts, I stick in my earbuds, pull out my phone, and find a playlist. The first track is one of my favorite artist collaborations. "Broken" by Seether and Amy Lee of Evanescence. She has the most beautiful voice, and paired with his, I could play the song on a loop.

Deep in my own piece of heaven, I rest against the window and stare at the passing scenery. There are wheat fields for as far as the eye can see. There are also large, beautiful, expensive-looking homes that sit on acres and acres of land.

Thomas told me many homes have landing strips for private airplanes. Or the homeowners store their planes at the small airport that sits between Delridge and Cambridge. Rich folks live in Cambridge and Delridge for two reasons—privacy and to get away from big-city living.

Along the way, the driver makes two more stops. Another young mom and her toddler get on the shuttle. Holding on to her little boy, the mom sits across from the other mom, and they start chatting. I can't hear what they're saying; my music is blasting. From the smiles on their faces, they must be friends.

On the last stop before the town center, a kid my age boards. He sits behind the driver with his back against the window and his arm resting on top of the seat. He stares at me. I stare back.

Dark-chocolate hair gelled into spikey strands.

Intense eyes framed by thick brows. His face is made up of sharp angles and strong lines. Sculpted by an angel, the finishing touches done by the devil.

He watches me with eyes hooded. The boy appears disinterested, but I don't let down my guard. Boys who look that dangerous are always aware of their surroundings, ready to pounce when an opportunity presents itself. They are the worst predators. They don't go in straight for the kill. They like to play with their prey first.

Danger and Disinterested is familiar, but I don't recall seeing him at Cambridge High. If he lives near the last stop, then he could be a student at Delridge High. The town center is not in the center of Cambridge, but closer to the border of Cambridge and Delridge.

After what seems like minutes of staring at one another, I glance away and check my messages. There's only one. It's from Thomas, asking how school is and do I need more money transferred into my account. I keep my answer short.

Me: Good. No.

I feel bad when he shoots back a message right away. His text was from three days ago.

Thomas: If there's anything you need, ask, okay?
Me: K

I plan on asking him if I can help around the estate, but that's a conversation and not a text. There's no point disturbing his vacation. I take out my earbuds and shove it and my cell into my bag. We're at the town center.

The boy doesn't get off first. Like me, he hangs back and waits for the women and their kids. I go next. Passing the driver and going down the steps, the back of my head tingles. The boy is staring again.

We get off on the side of the street that has a directory of the shops and the restaurants. For how small Cambridge and Delridge are, the town center is huge. I search the directory and find the restaurant.

No wonder Eleanor and I didn't walk by the restaurant when she brought me here to shop for clothes and shoes for school. The pho restaurant is at the far end of the town center, away from the high-end restaurants and boutiques.

I weave through the crowd. The pretty dresses in the window snag my attention, but I keep on walking, sparing the blue dress with the plunging neckline a fleeting glance.

The dress, made of tulle and lace and the straps dotted with flowers, must cost a grand or two. Money I don't have. Anyway, what reason would I have to wear a fancy dress like that? This isn't a fairy tale.

At the end of the street, I hit the button for the walk sign. The back of my head tingles again. The boy is following me. Great. The sky darkens, and the wind picks up. A sign? I stick my hands inside the pockets of my jacket and pull the edges closer to my core. The light is taking its time changing. The boy's gaze drops to the spot between my shoulders and goes low. Is he checking out my ass? I'm wearing cargo pants with these ridiculously deep pockets. Where else would a girl keep her mace and switchblade?

The cargo pants also mold to my ass like a second skin. My ass is my least favorite part of my body. It's too big. I don't fixate on my imperfections. There's yelling from my left. Did a driver piss off another driver in the roundabout? I look off to the side. A lap dog runs across the roundabout, its leash flapping. He's running like he's on an epic doggy adventure.

Crap! In the middle of the roundabout is a swarm of bushes. The leash will get caught in a branch and choke the poor dog. I dart across the street. Everything happens in slow motion. The end of the leash catches on a branch. He keeps on running. The leash pulls taut, reeling him back. Oh, God, he'll choke.

I lunge for him. Someone screams behind me. I look to the side. A car is careening toward me. I open my mouth. Nothing comes out. Something big hits me from behind, and the air is knocked from my lungs. I fly forward face first. See a bush of red berries and spiky leaves coming up fast in my line of sight. No, no, no. Strong arms wrap around my waist and anchor me against a solid chest.

I step forward and slam my elbow back, instinct driving me to act out. Before my elbow can make contact with my rescuer's gut, I'm turned around. Thick fingers grasp my chin and tip my face up. I stare into sapphire eyes marred by what I've seen in the eyes of the guy I stole a car from—ruthlessness with a hint of crazy. I haven't seen Maddox in a year, but his last words stick with me.

"Someday, I'll come for what's owed to me, and you'll have no choice but to comply."

I'm not in the business of being indebted to anyone, most of all someone as dangerous as Maddox Stassi. Now, I'm indebted to someone else.

"Thanks." I set my hands on his chest and put space between us.

The boy's eyes rove over my face, then zone in on

my mouth. What is it with guys and their fascination with my lips? Someone clears their throat behind us. He doesn't stop staring at my lips.

"Freak sakes, Red, let go of her already."

Let go? I glance down. The boy Red has a firm hold on my arms.

"Go away, Rue, and take your little dog with you. This isn't Kansas."

This boy's watched *The Wizard of Oz*?

I untangle from his hold and face the girl named Rue. She's holding the dog close to her chest. He whimpers, and she pets his head and runs her fingers through his fur. She's checking for injuries.

"We should get over to the other side before traffic picks up." She points in the direction of where she and the dog came from.

I ignore the boy behind me and point in the direction I was headed before my plans were derailed by a boy named Red, a girl named Rue, and a cute-as-pie ball of white fur.

"I'm headed to the pho restaurant."

"It's that way." She nods behind her.

"The directory says that way."

"Fuck's sake, listen to Rue. She knows this place inside and out. Restaurant moved, and the new location isn't updated on the directory."

"Oh, okay, thanks."

I follow Rue and run across the roundabout, Red close on my heels.

"Why are you tagging along?" He's at my side, so close, our fingers graze. I stick my hands inside my jacket pockets.

"Never seen you around here. You new?"

"Yes."

"Where you from?"

"Why the questions?"

"To get to know you better."

"Well, don't. I don't stay in one place long enough."

"Take a chance on me and Rue. We're good people. Right, Rue?"

"Good people? Ha! You're a Sterling, and Sterling boys are bad news all around."

"You're related to Malice Sterling?" No wonder Red looked familiar.

I keep walking. Rue doesn't. She stops in the middle of the sidewalk. I plow into her.

"Don't speak my cousin's name around Rue. She hates him."

Interesting.

"How come I've never seen you two at Cambridge High?"

"We go to Delridge."

I'm associating with Cambridge's rivals, am indebted to a Sterling, *and* I'm hanging out with a girl who hates one of Seven's best friends. If Seven ever finds out about this, he'll shit bricks. This is awesome!

I step around Rue and loop my arm through hers. Red takes a spot on my other side. I loop my arm through his too.

"Pick my pockets and there'll be hell to pay, short stuff."

At five foot five, I don't think of myself as short, but next to Red's six-foot-two body, he's not off with his remark.

"Why would you think I'd steal from you?"

"It's not stealing. I call it borrowing," Rue supplies.

Red barks laughter. "'Cause you and Rue are alike. You don't like anyone having the upper hand. Having saved your life, I have one over you. You'll want to even the score."

"Where have you two been all my life?"

They laugh. My steps lighten.

"Since you know me so well, does that mean I'm off the hook?"

"Uh-uh. It's not in me to give you a free pass."

The ruthless gleam I glimpsed in his eyes earlier.

"No worries. There'll be plenty of time to mess with you." I wink at him.

"I'm looking forward to it, short stuff." He leans into me, pushing me into Rue. Rue tips over sideways. Red yanks and straightens us out, pulling us away from the path of a trash bin.

"Name's Leigh."

"Nice to meet you, Leigh," Rue says. "So, pho, huh?"

"Yes. A fr—" I almost referred to Seven as my friend. "A *classmate* told me about the place."

Seven and I are not friends. We agree we're enemies. Except last night, he said "never just friends." What does that mean in Seven speak?

Sighing at how confused I am about my feelings for him, this hate to love, love to hate thing swirling in my core, I put aside thoughts of Seven and enjoy time with my newfound friends.

Yes, I can call Rue and Red "friends." One saved me, and the other is leading me to a restaurant that serves soups that remind me of my time with my parents.

"Hey, do you two by chance know of a place that's hiring? I need a job."

"I don't."

"I do. Come on." Rue steers us to a red-and-black building.

I read the sign. "Cambridge Auto Parts." I smile. Original.

Red opens the door for us. I follow Rue inside, admiring how long and thick her black hair is. The ends brush the small of her back. She's my height and thin. And unlike my lighter brown eyes, her eyes are so dark, it's like staring into the moonless, starless night sky.

"Rue, what nationality are you?"

"Korean. You?"

"Same."

"Sisters from another mother. Nice." She glances over her shoulder and smiles at me. I smile back.

We walk up to the counter. There's a handful of customers in the store. The smell of leather and pine permeates the air.

"Busy much?" Rue asks the guy behind the counter.

He's buff, with a buzz cut and a full beard. Tats line his neck. He looks up from whatever he's writing down on a piece of paper and rolls his eyes at Rue.

I like him instantly.

"Smart off much, Rue?"

"Is that your latest nickname for me? If it is, it's cute. Beats cockblocker."

Laughter from the guys in the windshield wiper aisle.

"What you did at that party was uncalled for."

"I saved you from catching a case of crabs," she says, her voice low so that only the four of us can hear. "Condoms don't save you from those critters, Mason."

"She has a point, man." Red rests his hip on the counter. He and Rue fist bump. These two. I bite down on my smile. They are a hoot.

"Leigh just moved here, and she's looking for a job. You said you need someone to help cover until Iris gets back from maternity leave."

Mason looks me up and down. "You know anything about cars and auto parts?"

"Enough to 'borrow' some guy's battery from his truck."

He smirks. "Great answer. You're hired."

I beam. "When can I start?"

"First off, are you a minor? Do you go to school with these rebels?"

A fitting name for Rue and Red.

"I go to Cambridge High."

"Then you're limited to eighteen hours a week."

"I'm working Fridays and Saturdays at Queenie's, but don't know total hours yet."

"Hand over your cell." He gestures for my phone.

I pull it out of my bag, unlock the screen, and give it to him.

"My number. Text me your schedule, and I'll see what I can do. You want to work the maximum eighteen?"

"Job's temporary, right?" I ask.

"Yeah. Iris gets back in three months."

"Then I'll work the maximum."

He reaches under the counter. When he straightens, he's holding a bunch of papers in his hand. "Fill these out. What size shirt do you wear?"

"Small."

"I'll have a uniform shirt ready for you. Wear black slacks. Got that?"

"Thank you." I extend my hand, and we shake on it.

On the way out, Red wraps his arms around my waist and Rue's. We walk to the restaurant with smiles on our faces, Rue's dog yapping away at everything in his or her line of sight.

"We're complete, Rue," Red says.

We stop in front of the door to the pho restaurant.

"You and me and Leigh, we are rebels."

"Outcasts," Rue says.

"A triple threat." I put in my two cents.

"Triple threat, I like that." Red nods, this slow up and down of his head. "To new beginnings." He sticks out his pinky finger. "To the triple threats."

Rue and I hook our fingers on his and say in unison, "To the triple threats."

I smile. Can't stop smiling as I share a meal with my new friends. I've never been happier.

17

SEVEN

I glance from the tree to my bedroom window to the wired fencing rolled up into a ball next to the side of the house. Why the groundskeeper put it there is beyond my understanding, but I see how Leigh hurt herself. She must've scraped the back of her leg on the metal points the night she stole my lucky coin and my gear.

I stroke my chin and return my attention to the tree. The lowest branch is high up. The other branches are spread out.

She would have to have a running start in order to jump high enough to grab on to that lowest branch. Then she'd have to reach high, hug the next branch, and with her legs wrapped around it, somehow pull herself up into a sitting position before starting over and repeating until she's in front of my window.

I shake my head. That girl is determined, crazy, brave, and . . . limber.

The front door opens and slams shut. My mom rushes out of the house and stomps off to her car. She's carrying luggage. My dad marches after her.

"I said we'd fucking talk, Emilia."

"You call that talking? We screamed at one another, Six."

I watch, helpless, as my parents' marriage unfolds into what-the-fuckery.

"Where you going?" He grabs her arm.

She yanks her arm from his grip. "Anywhere but where you're at."

Ouch.

"I'm done. *We're* done."

"Give me another chance."

"You had your chance to explain and you didn't. Why the hell was *she* in your hotel room?"

My dad opens his mouth. Shuts it. I kick at the ground. Damn him, why is it so difficult for him to open up to my mom lately when he never had a problem before? Or is he keeping his trap closed because that woman in his hotel room had something to do with his job?

My dad's line of work has to do with foreign trade. He won't get into the details, but he travels a lot. My hunch is what he does is super-agent secret shit, or he's a mobster. He looks more mobster than secret agent.

He's lined with muscles. Tatted. His sleeve tattoos are bold and frightening. Skulls. Snakes. The Grim Reaper prominent on his chest. Has a mean scar transecting his face from his right brow to the left corner of his mouth. He got in a bad knife fight. That's all he'll say. My mom says otherwise. She said he saved her life, and indebted to him, she agreed to marry him.

That's the spiel she gives me on how they met, but I doubt she just gave in and married my scarred, mean-ass father. My mother is beautiful, with her kind eyes and infectious laughter. Every time she laughs, which is less often these days, my dad stops what he's doing and stares at her.

I scram as soon as the heat level in the room goes from hot to sweltering hot. My parents, they are horndogs. Not lately, though. Lately, they've been sleeping in different rooms.

"Have your lawyer call mine. I don't want to see you again."

"The house, the cars, the money—"

"I don't want any of that, Six." She tosses the luggage into the back seat of her SUV.

"Anything. I'll give you anything, Emilia. Stay. Please."

She faces my dad. There are tears in my mother's hazel eyes. I can't decide who I hate more. My dad for making my mom cry. Or my mom for leaving us.

"I want the truth."

"You'll hate me."

"I hate you now."

"Emilia." He extends his hand to her.

She steps forward, then shakes her head. "We need time apart, Six. I'm sorry."

Mom rushes over to me and pulls me in for a hug.

"Take care of your father, Seven. I'll be in touch. I love you."

"I love you too." I don't hug her back. My arms hang at my sides. She's leaving us. Goddammit, she's *abandoning* us.

My chest aching, I step out of her hold and go stand by my father. I never wanted it to come to this.

For my parents to give up on something that brought them happiness.

It's all I remember growing up. My parents flirting, smiling, laughing. Them treating each day together as though it were their last. Now there's nothing.

Mom gets in the car and drives off without sparing us a glance in the rearview or sticking her hand out the window to wave at us. Normal things she did even when she did something as simple as returning to the grocery store for one dumb and giant onion for our burgers.

Can't have hamburgers without slices of sweet Walla Walla onions, she'd say with a smile while wiping away the tears pouring down her face. No matter what my mother did, refrigerate, nuke, put on dark shades, she always cried when cutting up onions.

"Shit, Son, what the fuck is wrong with me? I just let the best thing that's ever happened to me walk the fuck out of my life."

"She'll come back." She has to.

My dad has survived some bad shit in his past from my shooting the breeze with my cousins in Cali. My mom leaving? Yeah, I don't know if he'll survive that kind of devastation.

How did Leigh survive her parents' deaths?

Seven foster homes in five years?

Her life growing up in a shitty neighborhood?

I have to know.

That girl is brave and strong.

Defiant.

Doesn't take shit from anyone, including the biggest jerk of them all—me.

18

I lay in bed and think about my afternoon with Rue and Red. After I slurped up my pho, I filled out the paperwork Mason gave me.

When all of us were done eating and we paid, we headed back to the auto parts store, and I dropped off the paperwork. Then we did the fun stuff. Talking. Laughing. Window shopping. Red didn't want to be caught dead going into a clothing store with us girls, so we indulged him and stared at the well-dressed mannequins in the window.

I might have stared too longingly at the sapphire princess dress with the plunging neckline. Rue clasps her hands behind her back and rocks on her heels, looking from me to the dress.

"Size six, right?"

"How'd you guess?" I smirk.

She and I could be twins, except her eyes are deep pools of ink and mine are a light shade of brown. She gives me a cheeky smile.

"Homecoming is in a month. You have time to save up."

"Mason will be more than willing to give you hours," Red chimes in.

"We'll see." A lot can happen. And who would ask me to homecoming anyway? The students at Cambridge High hate me for talking back to their king.

Done with admiring a dress I could never afford, and even if I could, it isn't high enough on my list of priority purchases, I rush to the next window and make a mental list of the desserts I'd buy from Sweet Creations Two, a pun on too.

"Is there a Sweet Creations One?" I ask.

"In McMillan, a half hour from here. Same owner. He thought it'd be cool to have a one and a two."

"Are both things like the other or is one not like the other?" I ask, putting my spin on the lyrics from a Taylor Swift song.

From the way Red is looking at me, like I'm off

my rocker, he doesn't get my dumb attempt to be funny. Rue? Rue laughs in her hands.

"You are definitely my sister from another mother," she said. "Do you have sisters or brothers?"

"None. You?"

"My sister, Riley. She's a senior at DU."

"Does she like it there?"

"Not really. She's mainly there for the degree and her friends. They call themselves the Sass Squad. It's a play on Sasquatch."

"Like Big Foot?"

"Yep." She pulls out her phone from her back pocket and shows me a picture of her sister and the girls on the Sass Squad. "The one with light-brown hair is Gwen Bliss. Gwen's family owns a lavender farm in McMillan. Then there's Ever Moretti. Isn't she pretty? Her brown hair is borderline black, it's so dark. Her brother owns a tattoo shop. Next to her is Syn Winters. Is that not a sick name or what? And look at her piercings. Cool, right?"

I nod. I love the white-blonde girl with the pixie face's face piercings. Her bottom lip, nose, and right brow are pierced. I point to the last girls in the lineup.

"Is this your sister?"

"How'd you guess?" She smiles and crosses her eyes.

"Because you two could be twins." High cheekbones. Aristocratic nose. Small chin. Plump lips. What my dad would call kissable. He teased my mom all the time about her full lips.

"Next to her is Arie Kim. Arie has three siblings, and they and her all have different fathers."

Wow. "Why do they call themselves Sass Squad?"

Rue puts her phone away. "Freshman year, Gwen threw a Sasquatch party at her family's farm. She's superstitious and thought paying homage to the big guy in a place where there's been sightings would bring luck to her family, but no one came except for her roommates, Ever and Arie, and Riley and Syn who roomed together. That's how they all became friends. They're all sassy too."

"That's great." It is.

"You forgot to mention my brother." Red wedges between us, slings his arms over our shoulders, and steers us to the next shop.

It's a café. The boy wants coffee. I do too. I'd overslept and rushed out the door, shoveling food in my mouth. Yeah, not very ladylike.

"What about him?"

"That he's in Dumas too. He's keeping an eye on your sister. She has a bad habit."

Rue shoves Red's arm off her shoulder. "Don't destroy Leigh's opinion of my sister before she's formed them. Riley is the kindest person. She just needs a push in the right direction. That right direction is away from Midnight. Midnight is an ass."

"Hey, that's my brother you're speaking of."

"Then don't be so hard on my sister, making her out to be this bad person when she's not."

They're arguing in the middle of the sidewalk. People are staring. I put my hands on their arms. "Hey, we all have our flaws and our bad days. I'm sure they're nice people, and I can't wait to meet them. Thank you for telling me about them and showing me a picture of your sister and her friends. I like putting faces to the names."

Rue heaves a big sigh.

Red shoves his fingers through his hair.

"Do you know what this old lady, we call her Grandma Chu, used to do when kids fought?"

"No, what?" Rue narrows her eyes.

Red crosses his arms over his chest.

"She made them hug for a minute."

"I'm not hugging her."

"No way am I hugging him."

"It's sixty seconds. You can endure touching one another for sixty seconds. That's like dropping a piece of chocolate on the floor, picking it up on the basis of the five-second rule times twelve drops and pick ups."

They look at me like I'm snorting coke or smoking a bud in public. Which I've never done.

"Are you for real?" Red asks.

"Yes or no?"

"She is. You are my best guy friend." Rue smiles and opens her arms. "How about it?"

He steps into her arms, and they hug. I set the timer on my phone. People stare. After a minute, the two break apart with cheesy grins on their faces.

"Was that so bad?"

"It wasn't," Rue admits. "Your turn. Hug Red."

For funsies, I give in and hug Red. He is lean muscle. Tall. Smells nice too. But my body up against his does nothing for my girl parts. Not like how my body heats from the inside out when Seven is in proximity.

Many shops later, Red and I said goodbye to Rue. We exchanged numbers. At my stop, I hop off the shuttle and rushed home, feeling like I was running on clouds. I had a new job to get ready for, working alongside one of the nicest guys.

When I showed up for my three-to-eight shift at Queenie's, Miles handed me a royal-blue apron and a shirt with the diner's logo on it. Guess what it is? It's a pink crown with a Q in black at the point of the crown.

I told Miles the crown is pretty.

He said I'm prettier.

I rolled my eyes.

He laughed and rubbed his knuckles into the top of my head, messing up my topknot. That butt. I was so excited and happy, I sent a selfie of me wearing the uniform shirt to Rue and Red. Rue sent back hearts. Red texted back that I look smoking hot— can I do a strip tease for him, please? Um, no. What a flirt!

"What you smiling big for?"

I scream. My hand slams against the spot over my heart.

"Crap, Seven, you scared me." I hop off the bed and smack him across the shoulder. Bad idea. He curls his fingers around my wrist and tugs. I tip forward. He steps into my personal space until his body presses into mine.

"Why the shit-eating grin, Leigh? Did you meet someone you like?"

The way he says the last sentence, with this hot possessiveness . . . My heartbeat accelerates, and my mouth goes dry.

"Why do you ask?"

"A girl only smiles like that when a guy gives her something good."

"As if." I push at him. He doesn't budge.

"Tell, Leigh."

"Or else what?" I tip my chin at him.

"Or else I teach you a lesson. You're mine to harass."

"Harass? Is that what you call this middle-of-the-night sneaking in through my window you're doing?"

"What else would you call it?"

"Creeping."

"Creeping, harassing, it's all the same to me. Now, tell, Leigh. I want his name."

"No."

"No?"

"Uh-uh," I say.

"Okay, don't say I didn't warn you."

He lets go of my wrist and pushes me back. I fall onto the bed. Annoyed that I let him push me down,

I rise to a sitting position, but Seven gets on top of me and straddles my hips.

"Seven."

"Tell, Leigh."

"No."

"*Defiance.*"

"No, Seven. Geez. Leave it alone, already."

"So it was a guy."

"I didn't say it was."

"Why are you protecting him?"

I glance from his thick thighs holding me down to his face. "I could put in a good guess."

"Wrong answer." He leans forward, and holding his weight off me with his arms alongside my head, he stretches his body over mine and nuzzles my neck.

His warm breath on my skin, his nose dragging along my flesh . . . Heat licks up my spine. I wrap my legs around his waist and tip up my hips, cocooning the erection under his jeans in my hot spot.

"Leigh, *fuck.*"

I hold him tighter to me with my arms and my legs. His groan reverberates against my skin.

"Why are you here, Seven?"

"You know the answer."

His breath is minty, and he smells clean, like

clothes fresh out of the dryer. He must've showered and brushed his teeth. I turn into him, smush my face into his damp hair, and inhale his scent.

"Mmm, you smell good." Did I say that out loud?

"That so?" Smile in his voice.

"So. I could eat you up." Oh, God, I gotta stop thinking out loud.

"*Leigh*. Fuck."

He rolls off me and pulls me into his arms. Not sure what to do with my hands, I shift onto my side and stretch my arm across his chest.

"How was your day? Do anything fun?"

"That's all you have to say after your boner-inducing comment?"

"The one about eating you up?"

Groaning, he adjusts the front of his pants. "You're a little shit, you know that?"

He reaches for the remote and hits the "on" button. The panel on the ceiling opens. Raindrops pelt the windowpane. He takes off his shoes and his hoodie, and we crawl under the covers. I scoot close to the wall. He has other ideas. Seven grabs me around the waist and tugs me on top of him.

I look down into the sad eyes of an angel while rain falls from the heavens.

"That bad, huh?" My chest constricting, I cup his jaw and stroke my thumb over his warm skin.

His jaw tightens beneath my touch.

"Want to talk about it?" I fold my arms on his chest and rest my chin on my arms.

He shakes his head.

"What would you rather do?"

"You." His voice is low, husky.

"We're not friends, so a friends-with-benefits thing can't start between us."

"How about an enemies-with-benefits arrangement instead?" He runs his knuckle over my bottom lip.

His touch is gentle, but the way he's looking at me promises something on the rougher side. Like teeth raking over skin, tongue sucking on tongue, nails digging into flesh.

My breaths come out in spurts. The place between my legs throbs. I have this urge to touch myself. To take his hand and have him touch me too. Embarrassed at how easily he undoes me with one simple touch on my lip, I look away. He grasps my chin between his fingers and brings my face back to his.

"Well?"

"Whether we're friends or enemies or

acquaintances, I can't, Seven." I give him the same reason I gave Red. "I don't stick around one place long enough to have a friendship, a relationship, or a rivalry."

"Bullshit. For the right person, for the right reason, you would."

I start rolling off him. He slings his arm across my back and keeps me in place.

"You don't know me," I murmur.

"Give me that chance."

"Why, so you can mess with my head and my heart? No, thank you."

"Have you?"

"Have I what?"

"Fallen in love?"

"That's none of your business."

He searches my face. Wipes at the strands of hair falling across my forehead. "You're mine, Leigh, and that makes it my business."

"You're full of yourself."

"And you are fooling yourself if you think I'll let you go so easily."

I growl low in the back of my throat. He shifts us until I'm blinking up at him. Seven shoves his fingers in my hair. His other hand clamps on to my thigh.

"Have you ever fallen in love, Leigh?" His fingers press into my skin through my pajama bottoms.

It's not painful. What he does, the gentle press and release, press and release is sheer torture, and I'm on the verge of taking off my pants so that he can touch my skin.

"No," I admit, breathless. "You?"

He locks his gaze on mine. "Never."

"Allison?" A jolt of jealousy grabs at my core and I scold myself. Seven might say I'm his, but he never said he's mine. I'm a temporary fascination. A shiny new toy to pass his time with. The reason I should never let down my guard with him.

"When I say never, I mean it."

"Just checking."

"Anything else you'd like to know? 'Cause I'd like the guy's name now."

"No, and I'm not giving it to you."

"Why the hell not?"

"You can't mess with him, Seven. He's not someone to screw with."

"Don't tell me this guy goes to Delridge? I'll fuck him up when I get ahold of him."

"There's one problem. You don't have his name."

"I have my ways, Leigh."

"Why are you so possessive?"

"I'm keeping you safe from guys more dangerous than me."

"Why would a guy be interested in me when there are prettier girls?"

I think of Rue. Hannah too. She's gorgeous, with legs that go on and on, caramel-color hair that falls past her shoulders, deep green eyes, and she has an eye for fashion. Plus, she's popular with the guys and the girls, though she's been mean-girling as all get out.

"There are guys who like a girl with attitude. You have so much of it, you could light up a stadium."

"Ha-ha, not."

"I'm being serious, Leigh. Guys like that want to cage you, bringing you out only so they can break you of your defiance. It's how they get off."

"How is what you're doing different from what you claim they'll do to me?"

"I don't want to cage you. You can do whatever the hell you want so long as you give me your loyalty."

"You also want my obedience. Something I'll never give. I have my own opinions and ways of doing things. No one will break me of that."

"You won't put aside your ways even for love?"

"I don't bow down to a guy, not even for love."

"Brutal."

"Twenty-first-century mindset."

"So eating me is out of the question?"

I can't help it. I stick out my tongue and cross my eyes. "I wasn't literal, Seven. You smell good enough to eat, but I am not putting my mouth on any part of your body except for your yummy lips."

"My lips are yummy?"

"Delish," I say.

Smiling, he gets off me, flops onto his back, and crooks his finger. "Come here."

My gaze roams over his body, from his tousled hair to the way his shirt stretches over his impressive torso, to how well his jeans hug his hips and his long legs.

I shake my head. "It's a bad idea."

"I thought you weren't scared of me," he challenges.

"I'm not. Scared has nothing to do with bad ideas."

"Leigh, you're stubborn."

"And you only want to feel me up."

"Guilty."

Ugh, why couldn't he have denied it? It would make kicking him out of my place, demanding he go out the way he came, so much easier. Except I like having Seven here. He's fun to talk with. Hot to look at. And seeing the sadness in his eyes earlier still hurts me like a punch to the chest. Maybe if I give in, he'll give in too and tell me what's wrong.

"Are you planning on staying the night?"

"Hell yeah."

"Then take off your clothes. I don't plan on hearing you sawing logs again, Seven. The last time left me exhausted and grumpy."

"Ladies first. All of it, Leigh."

"I . . . I have scars."

"Fuck the scars. Any imperfection on you is a turn on, Beautiful Defiance."

"I'm beautiful?" No one's said that about me.

"Like a siren luring me to my watery grave."

I laugh. "Romantic, big guy."

"I'm not. Remember, I'm the predator, you're the prey. I want to toy with you, ravish you, eat you up."

His stare is intense and his words hot, searing my flesh. The nervousness returns. I'm in over my head. Messing with a boy I shouldn't mess with. He'll use me up, every last ounce of my emotions, then toss me aside when he's done toying and ravishing me.

"What are we getting ourselves into, Seven?"

"Don't think too hard on it, Defiance. But if it

doesn't feel right, tell me to go the fuck away, and I will. I won't stop by in the middle of the night again."

"That's the thing. It feels completely right. I like having you here with me."

"Then what are you waiting for? I'd love to see your imperfections, beautiful."

Turned inside out by the heat in his voice and his earnestness, I grab my camisole by the hem and tug it over my head. Sharp intake of breath from Seven. Self-conscious, I cross my arms over my small breasts.

"Take your arms away, Leigh."

The heat in his voice intensifies. As does the intensity in his gaze, the soft glow from the outside lights around the guesthouse shining in through the part in the curtains.

Is that the reason I left the lights on instead of turning them off like normal? I had a feeling Seven would sneak into my room?

He sits up and yanks off his shirt. My gaze roves over his wide shoulders, the sprinkle of dark chest hair across his pecs, the ridges of his six-pack abs, and the strip of hair disappearing inside his jeans. My attention hangs and lingers on the outline of his erection. Thick, long. I swallow down my nervousness.

If he thinks I'm beautiful, I'd say he's stunning, and I tell him so.

"A guy is stunning, eh?" He lunges forward, slides his hands under my arms, and gets me on top of him.

His chest hair brushes my breasts. My nipples pebble. Seven pulls the covers over us. His hands go low, and his fingers trace the lines etched into my skin.

"Whoever did this better be doing hard time. My dad's got connections to the underworld. One word from me and he'll send men after the fucker."

I weave my fingers into his chest hair and puff out a breath. "It wasn't one guy but a group of them. They held me down and did things to me."

"If you're speaking of rape, they're dead men."

"They didn't. Two officers on patrol stopped them before they could get to that point."

"What'd they beat you with?"

"An electrical cord."

"These scars are the reason you didn't want the nurses stripping you of your top."

"Yes," I admit.

"And your panties? What scars are you hiding, beautiful?"

"Seven, please, don't ask to see them."

"I'm not asking and never will you beg again.

Take them the fuck off, Leigh. I want a good reason to send men after those bastards."

I slide off him, get on my back, and remove my pajama bottoms and underwear. Seconds tick by. The bed on Seven's side dips. He tosses the covers off, and going low, he cups my hips and drops kisses on the words carved into my skin by guys who saw me as nothing but a pain in their asses when I demanded they stop selling drugs and alcohol to the kids on my block.

"You're not a snitch. Or the C word. You're beautiful. Every part of you."

His hot breath whispers across my skin, touching a part of me I've never shown to a guy. After he showers kisses on my scars, he finds my underwear buried under the covers, tugs them on me, and then rests his head on my belly. His hair tickles my skin.

"Did your parents love one another, Leigh?"

"Very much."

"Did they fight?"

"Like a rabid dog and a cat going through catnip withdrawal."

His muffled laughter on my skin tickles even more, and I squirm beneath his mouth.

"Great analogy."

"Thank you." I sift my fingers into his hair. "Beats your helium balloon one."

"No doubt."

This time, I laugh.

"What'd they fight over?"

"Small things like who got the bigger slice of apple pie, both their favorite pie. Or who got the most meatballs in their pho. Usually my mom did. The owner of the restaurant that my father worked for loved my mother. My mother made the prettiest dresses for her granddaughters, and they all went off and married these wealthy businessmen. She said she owed their luck to my mom's eye-catching, beautiful dresses."

"They didn't fight over crap like finding a woman in your father's hotel room?" He untangles my fingers from his hair, gets out of bed, and puts his shirt back on. "Never mind. I should go."

I prop myself on my elbows. "Stay. Please."

"I said not to beg or ask for a favor unless you're willing to work for it or am willing to give up something in return."

He's angry. Embarrassed, too, for showing me the vulnerable side of himself. A side that cares enough about his parents' marriage to ask a girl he barely knows about her parents'.

I reach for my camisole and pull it over my head. To say my next piece, I need to *not* be vulnerable. Vulnerable is being half-naked.

"A kiss. I'll give you a kiss if you'll stay the night with me."

"A kiss on the corner of our mouths won't convince me."

"A full-on-the-mouth kiss with tongue, Seven. That's what I meant. Satisfied?" I glower, fully understanding he can see me.

Or, he hears the annoyance in my tone.

"Yeah. Yeah, I am." He gets under the covers, and with his back resting against the headboard, he pats his lap. I straddle his thighs.

"Before we kiss, I want us to talk."

"Why?"

"Because that's what two people who will never be just friends do."

"Fine." He tips his head back and bounces it off the headboard in this irksome tap, tap, tap.

I stop the irksome motion with my palms to the sides of his head, and tipping forward, I tell him of my mother's deal with Tony. Seven then spills his parents' argument before his mother left his father standing there looking after her with hurt on his face.

"What if your dad's situation is like my mom's? What if he was set up? What if someone is blackmailing him?"

"How would we know if he was?"

"I have someone I can contact, but promise you'll be fine with whatever he asks of me? I owe him for saving my life."

"How many lives do you have?"

"Must be a lot. I was almost run over in this crazy roundabout trying to save a dog."

"What? Are you okay?" He runs his palms up and down my arms. Pats my sides and my thighs too.

I bite down on my bottom lip, unhinged by his concern.

"I'm fine. Should I get ahold of him? I stole his car, so he might not want anything to do with me."

Maddox won't be thrilled, but he'll like hearing from me. It'll give him the chance to even the score for him saving my life from that car of his I wrecked. He pulled me out of it right before a semi truck plowed into the driver side.

"Wait, the grand theft auto charge, you stole this dude's car?"

"It wasn't an average 'car' but a limited edition Bugatti."

Seven's eyes get big. "Those things go for close to three fucking million. *Millions*, Leigh."

I scowl. "I know how much one costs. Maddox reminded me over and over of the price tag, okay?"

"Maddox. What's the dude's last name?"

"Um, Stassi."

"Double fuck me. You stole *Mad* Maddox's Bugatti?"

"I take it you've heard of him?"

"He made headlines for ordering the castration of the men who raped his little sister."

"*Alleged* castration," I say.

"Alleged my ass. The public ate up his vigilante act. Why involve ourselves with that dangerous fucker?"

"He's good on his word and has connections."

"He'll do this for you why? Did you two do the dirty?"

"I never slept with him."

"You let me sleep with you."

"Are you for real?"

"Say what you mean, Leigh, and I will be as real as the scars on your body."

"Fine. I'm a virgin. Satisfied?"

"More than you'll ever know."

What he says, how he says it. Like it's the most

special thing in the world. Like it means so much to him that I haven't been with a guy.

"I . . . Seven."

Undone, I press my mouth on his. Move my lips side to side. His lips are soft. His hold on my hips is firm. One peck. Two pecks. Closed mouth kisses.

"Leigh." My name is murmured on my lips, and hot from the inside out, I nudge his mouth open with my tongue.

He is sweet and warm, and our kiss full on the mouth is everything I imagined it would be, starting off slow and tentative then cresting into this intensity that sets me afire from my head to my toes. Moaning, I shove my fingers in his hair and slant his head. I deepen the kiss and grind on his erection.

I rock back and forth along his thickness beneath his jeans. He feels so good. His mouth on mine, his length and thickness rubbing my pussy through our clothes, my arousal clinging to my panties with every back and forth motion from me.

"Leigh, babe, God, you're fucking beautiful."

He tips us forward and gets me on my back. I stretch out my legs. Resting on one hip, he kisses a path down my neck, lifts my camisole and takes a nipple in his mouth.

His wet warm mouth on my hardened bud,

nipping and sucking . . . I come off the bed. Clamp his head to my breast. His laughter muffles against my skin, and my toes curl. *They curl.*

"Seven, that feels so good, but we should stop."

"Agree."

"Wait, you do?" I lift my head and look at him.

"Leigh, we agreed on a kiss. This is rounding second base."

"You're right."

"Hold up. Say that again."

"Wipe that shit-eating grin off your face, Seven Shanahan."

"Leigh."

"Okay, fine, you are right. Right, right, right. Happy?"

"Over the moon. Cool. You're cool, Defiance."

"Thanks." I smile, liking our easy back and forth. It's never been this easy talking to a guy.

Seven hops out of bed, takes off his clothes except for his boxers, and crawls back under the covers. We snuggle. Yep, we snuggled after that hot-as-sin heavy petting.

"You'll get ahold of Maddox?" He slides his arm across my shoulder, under my mass of long hair.

"First thing tomorrow morning." I curl my body into his.

"You'll tell me what he says?"

"His exact words, Seven."

"And those fuckers who messed with you? Want me to fuck them up?"

"No need." I cradle his face with my palm. Tilt his head away from me. Kiss the underside of his jaw. "They're dead."

"Maddox?"

"Mum's the word. I'm not a snitch."

"Gotcha. Night, Leigh."

"Goodnight, Seven. Thank you for staying."

"Pass up your boner-inducing kisses? Never, Defiance."

I laugh. "So romantic, Seven. So romantic."

19

*O*n Monday, it's back to the status quo at school. I stay out of Seven's way until the last bell rings. Then I trudge to his football practice, not looking forward to sitting on my duff out in the cold and on metal bleachers wet from the rain.

At the gate to the football field, I hitch my backpack higher on my shoulder, tug the hood of my jacket over my head, and open my umbrella.

This girl is going incognito.

I find a semi-dry spot on the bleachers, wipe off any leftover wetness with my sleeve, and sit. The boys are practicing on the field. The cheerleaders are in the gym. Hannah avoids me like I have a contagious disease, but her avoidance doesn't stop her from openly glaring at me during lunch.

We have the same lunch period. She sits at the table reserved for cheerleaders. In front and behind their table is half the football team. The other half has the other lunch period. Lucky me, Seven also has the same lunch period.

He ignores me too. Except he doesn't glare or stare or do anything that resembles interest or hate. Not toward me anyway, but Ginger? He goes over to the cheerleaders' table and talks to her. Makes her laugh. Has her touching his arm in this intimate way that has me wanting to rush over and yank out her hair.

Him showering her with attention has me disappointed and hurting after what happened between us this weekend. But I don't forget my promise to help him with his parents' situation. I called Maddox and left a message.

He hasn't returned my call, and I'm not surprised. He's probably taking part in an orgy of epic proportions, cutting off more guys' dicks who dare mess with him and his family, or he's adding more million-dollar sportscars to his collection.

I rest my elbows on my knees, and setting my chin in my palm, I blow out a breath. Being right sucks. I'm a new toy, and that's why Seven swindled me into giving him a piece of my heart when I told him of my parents and life back home in Oakland.

I should regret telling him those personal things. Or letting him see and kiss on my scars. Or let what he did mean something to me; that gets my heart pitter-pattering every time I think of us talking and touching while rain pitter-patters on the skylight. But I have no regrets. And what he did and said means the world to me.

The wind picks up, and I fold into myself and hold the umbrella closer to my head. A shrill ringing cuts into the silence. I hold on to the umbrella handle with one hand and fumble in my backpack for my phone with the other.

I glance at the screen. It's not Maddox. The call is from an unknown number. What if it's Eleanor? What if something happened to Thomas?

I answer. "Hello?"

"Leigh?"

"Um, yes, who is this?"

"Leigh, it's me, Henry."

Growling, I hang up on him.

He calls right back, again and again. After the fourth time and Seven's coach glowering at me, I pick up the call.

"What do you want, Henry?"

"Look, Leigh, I'm sorry if I hurt you. I feel bad."

"You're apologizing because *you* feel bad? I came down with pneumonia from swallowing pool water. Was admitted overnight."

"Shit. Send me the bill."

One problem out of the way.

"Again, what do you want?"

"To ask a favor. I'll understand if you say no. You didn't exactly accept my apology."

He gets me on a technicality, and now *I'm* the one feeling guilty? "Apology accepted," I begrudgingly tell him.

"Thank God. It was all I thought about, Leigh. You could have died."

"No shit, Sherlock."

He laughs. A hint of a smile curls my mouth.

"The favor?"

"Keep an eye on Hannah at this party she's going to on Thursday."

What is it with these kids and partying on a school night?

"She's been partying since you and your parents left. What's so special about this one?"

"The place where it's being held at. Brody goes to Delridge. His girlfriend, Cambridge. Kids from both schools will be there, including players from the football teams. Brody plays for the Daredevils."

I blow at my nails painted Gypsy Ink. "I'm not in the habit of breaking up fistfights."

"That's not why I need you there. Brody's older brothers are pervs. They like their girls young. You have a good head on your shoulders. Won't let anyone mess with you. I've seen the mace and the switchblade you're packing."

"How—"

"I'm sorry, Leigh. I went through your bag when my dad showed you the guesthouse."

"You're a jerk."

"Does that mean you'll do it?"

"Parties aren't my scene."

"Go for Hannah and the scavenger hunt."

"There's a *scavenger hunt?*"

"Winner gets the bag of money."

"How big is this bag? Is it lunch-bag size?"

"King pillowcase."

"I'm in." The money will go toward my buy-Leigh-a-car fund.

"Thanks, Leigh. I appreciate it."

"Sure." I'm ready to hang up, but there's this tightness in my chest. Henry trusts me to watch over

Hannah. Said I have a good head on my shoulders and that I'm one tough cookie.

"Henry?"

"Yeah?"

"I'm sorry for what I said that night you came home."

"I deserved it. I had no right speaking to you like that. It's just . . . It's been a rough couple weeks at school, so no worries, okay? Don't worry your pretty head about anything you say to me, Leigh. You're family now."

My heart does a somersault in my chest. Does Henry know of mine and Thomas's secret?

"Thanks, Henry. I'll talk to you later."

"Later, Leigh."

Smiling, I tuck my cell inside my backpack. Little did I know my happiness is easily wiped away by Seven's assery.

20

"*H*ey, why's New Girl here? Does she think we'll give her the time of day if she sits there and *ogles* us?"

Ogle? As if.

Seven's teammate points at me and sneers. His sneers aren't confusing in this mix of menacing and holy hotness way that Seven's is. This jerk's sneer is ugly, and his words, rude.

I take the steps on the bleachers one by one, holding on to the railing for support. The steps are slippery, and with my crappy luck, I'll slip and fall on my ass in front of the entire football team. Chatter floats from behind me on my way down. The cheerleaders are done with practice.

With my feet on solid ground, I head for Seven.

He cups the back of his head and looks down at the ground. I stop walking toward him and pivot in the direction of the school's parking lot, his embarrassment dawning on me.

His teammates don't know that he's failing his classes and is on the verge of being benched. I feel bad for him, but at the same time, I'm irritated too. Is it a blow to his ego to admit he's not doing his best because he royally messed up? My guess is a solid yes. Seven is the type of guy who doesn't like to admit his mistakes, his defeats and failures, or that he needs help.

"Where the hell are you going, fresh meat? Don't you want some something, something?"

I keep on walking. Best not to rile up the jerk with my resting bitch face. Or to see him doing the pelvic thrust, his way of showing me his "something, something."

A deep voice cuts into the thick-with-tension silence. "Don't speak to her that way, shithead. She's with me."

No, it's not Seven coming to my defense. He has too much pride. Malice walks over and slings his arm across my shoulders. He smells of sweat and grass and the cool air.

"Thanks for waiting, babe."

Babe? I open my mouth; I'm not his girl. Malice squeezes my shoulder and says near my ear, "Play along. I'm helping you and Seven."

I like the words help, you, and Seven. I take a deep breath, relieved Malice isn't a total jerk, and catch a whiff of sweat and body odor. I wrinkle my nose.

"Shouldn't you hit the locker room first and change out of the wet uniform?"

He sniffs his armpit. "Nah, I'm good."

"You own a GT-R," I sputter. "Beauty shouldn't be tainted with boy BO and sweat."

"Boy?" He throws back his head and laughs. "I'm no boy, Leigh. I am all man."

To make his point, he reaches down and grabs his crotch. I roll my eyes.

"Okay, champ."

"A champ who wants a piece of you, sweet thing."

We've progressed from babe to sweet thing? Wow, he's laying it on thick. And what high school boy speaks like he's a college dude?

Or Malice is getting someone's boxers in a bunch. There's a low growl from behind us. The guys and the cheerleaders crowd us as we make our way to Malice's GT-R. There's crackling in the air, like a clap of thunder before lightning strikes.

There's also this silent chant, "Fight, fight, fight," trailing behind us.

I cluck my tongue. Kids and their thirst for blood and drama.

"You must have it bad for her," the jerk says. "Never heard laughter from that cocky mouth of yours."

"Yeah, I got it bad. Now, piss off. My girl and I need alone time." He unlocks the car doors and holds the passenger-side door open for me. I slide inside. The smell of leather is strong.

Malice throws his backpack and gear in the back and climbs in, his large body taking up considerable space.

"Nice ride." I cup the top of the gear stick. "I love manuals."

"You know how to drive one?"

"Not really. I crashed my first. It was a three-million-dollar lapse in judgement."

His eyes widen. "What'd you wreck?"

"A Bugatti." My voice goes up a notch.

"Holy fuck. What'd the owner do?"

"Brought charges of grand theft auto on me."

"Double holy fuck. And totally cool." He sticks his fist out. We fist bump.

Seven and Trace watch us from their spot next to

Seven's pickup truck. Trace says something out the side of his mouth to Hannah and the other cheerleaders. Ginger is on the other side of Seven, her pale skin and light blonde hair contrasting nicely with Seven's dark looks. Pitch black hair. Bottomless pool of ink colored eyes. Dark scowl on his pretty face.

Seven catches us looking his way, and he puts his thumb and index finger together, apart, together, apart. Is he "squeezing" our heads? God, he can be so immature. I glower.

Malice tips his head at Seven. "You helping him out of his troubles? Is that the reason you're sitting out in the cold and rain? You waiting for Seven?"

I glance away from Seven's death glare. "I plead the fifth."

"Hey, if it helps you sleep better at night, I won't pester or judge. But watch from inside my car, okay?"

"Can't." I promised Seven never to be indebted to a Sterling.

"You're giving up the chance to sit inside this fine piece of machinery?"

"Much to my annoyance, yes."

"It's Seven, isn't it?"

"You know me too well."

He laughs. "I'd like to get to know you better."

"No can do."

"Again, Seven?"

"Copy that."

He laughs again. "You're a hoot."

I give him a slight nod of my head and a smile. "Why, thank you."

He ducks his head. His wide shoulders shake. He slides his eyes back up to mine, and wow, the dimpled smile on his face . . . My cheeks heat. Malice should smile more.

"Can I say anything that will have you switching to Team Malice?"

"And here I thought you were a grumpy puss with absolutely zero humor." Is that the reason Rue dislikes Malice?

He reaches for my hand and drops a kiss on my knuckles. "For you, I'd hang up my grumpy puss boots and give you the funnies."

"Brooding is sexier."

"You can have that too. Every part and piece of me. What do you say?" His eyes twinkle.

"He's watching us, isn't he?" I ask.

"With a laser-beam focus that can slice this ride in half."

"Nice."

He shakes his head and laughs. "You should know better than to mess with Seven. He can be a mean mother-effer."

"Thanks for the warning."

"You sure you won't change your mind?" He stares at my mouth.

"I'm certain."

"He's lucky you have his back, Leigh."

Before I realize what's happening and can put a stop to it, Malice clasps my head in his palms, pulls me close, and plants a kiss on the top of my head. I close my eyes, wishing it were Seven instead. The car shakes. There's pounding on my window. I turn, and the cliché of if looks could kill . . . The expression on Seven's face would slice and I'd bleed red.

Malice doesn't give Seven another chance to mess with his sportscar. He cranks the engine and peels out of the parking lot.

"Did I get him in the nuts with the rocks that fell from his truck's chassis?"

I glance in the side mirror. "He's upright and not grabbing at his crotch."

"That fucker. It'll take a full-body assault to take him down."

Brutal, but Malice is wrong. It only took the

threat of his parents' marriage failing to wound Seven. His mom leaving his dad cuts deep, and I won't let him continue to hurt.

I'll help him even if what goes on in my room doesn't go past the walls.

Seven says I'm his, but he never said he's mine.

Big difference.

21

SEVEN

*S*eething, I watch Malice drive off with Leigh. I get in my truck, ignoring Hannah and her curiosity. She's been asking a shit ton of questions lately since that comment of Leigh's, the one demanding I put a sock on my snoring.

Between classes, Hannah pestered me for what happened the night Henry came home. Said Henry's friend posted something on social media about drowning a rat in the Stevenson pool. As far as she's concerned, they don't have a rat problem.

I can think of a handful of rats I'd like to exterminate. One of them being my dickwad teammate John for giving Leigh a hard time. The second rat is Malice for saying Leigh is *his* girl. Third rodent is Henry. No explanation needed. And, I've saved the best rat for last.

I'm a rat bastard for not speaking up for Leigh. A coward for not owning up to my mistakes. I'm also a sorry excuse of a leader.

As soon as John opened his mouth, I should have put a nail in that bastardly coffin and put him in his place for talking trash to a girl who's done nothing wrong other than to help a guy from failing his classes.

Hanging my head, I turn the ignition, shift the truck into gear, and make my way home.

On the driveway that'll get me to the house, I make a U-turn and park my truck alongside the fence separating the two properties. I have the house to myself. Dad is MIA. He was gone when I woke this morning. During lunch period, he texted saying he'd be gone for the week.

Did he find out where Mom is staying? Is he with her now, talking sense into her? It's what I wanted to text back, but I kept my text short.

Me: K

Leigh's right. I have been distracted. Have been getting into fights. Anything to get rid of the ball of aggression building in me since I overheard my mom accusing Dad of cheating on her. I've been there, except me and Allison weren't marriage-vow serious.

Yeah, it pissed me off that she cheated. I should've had the good sense to end things between us before it got to that point. Instead, I let her talk me into keeping our lifeless relationship going.

Mom and Dad, though?

They made *vows*.

I grab my backpack, get out of my truck, and don't bother locking the doors. There's no chance anyone will steal the old girl. The only local thief I know of is home. I bypass knocking on the front door and go in through the open window.

"Leigh, if Malice is in there with you, you better tell him to scram or I'll fuck up his pretty face." I drop my backpack on the floor and climb inside, shutting the window behind me.

"Such language." She tsks. "He's not here."

She's sitting on the bed, looking sexy as fuck in a pair of those yoga pants girls love to wear and us guys love seeing them wear. On the front of her gray T-shirt are the words, "Got Buns?" Below the writing is a picture of Princess Leia.

"Did he stick around?"

"Are you really asking if he stuck around long

enough to stick his tongue in my mouth or his junk in me?"

"Leigh, fuck's sake, you and your mouth." I cram my hands in my pockets and pull my shoulders inward. "Well, did he?"

"No. He dropped me off and didn't let anything go further. He's a gentleman."

I scoff. "A Sterling is far from being decent. Remember that."

I take my hands out of my pockets, grab my notebooks and textbooks from my backpack, and strew everything, including my body, on Leigh's bed.

"Why do you have an off opinion of Sterling guys, including Malice? Did they give you a wedgie or one too many knuckle sandwiches?"

"Not funny, Leigh. And yeah, one of them crossed me. He's the douchebag Allison cheated on me with. Thing is, she's telling me she doesn't remember going with him into one of the bedrooms at this party our junior year."

"She was raped? Did she go to the police?"

"She's ashamed as fuck, Leigh. Blames herself for what happened. She told me last week."

"I . . . I'm sorry, Seven. I see why you don't like the Sterlings."

"They're a tight family. Huge too. They propagate

like rabbits in heat."

She scrunches her face. "Ugh, the imagery. What will I do without the images you put in my head?"

I'd like to put other dirty images in her head. Ones of us fucking like rabbits. In every position my horny eighteen-year-old mind can come up with.

"Does that mean you forgive and forgot what happened at practice?"

Rolling off my back and onto my stomach, I talk my dick down from its erect pose. It's uncomfortable as fuck when I'm trying to have a serious talk with Leigh.

"If you promise not to mess with Malice's face, I will. I'm partial to his face. He's very handsome. Must be his perpetual scowl."

"*Leigh.*" Have I mentioned I hate that fucker and his scowl?

"Promise, Seven."

Why do I have the gut feeling she's got something up her sleeve? I give her my promise. We have a shit ton of catching up to do, and this business with Malice is holding up the show. Not to mention, talking about the Sterlings gets me in a foul mood fast.

"Pinky swear." She crawls to me on her hands and knees and sticks her face near mine.

I reach up and pull down her bottom lip. Run the pad of my thumb over the cut that's healed.

"What happened, Leigh?"

She tips back and sits with her legs tucked under her ass. "If I tell, I would have to give up someone else's secret, and I can't do that. I'm sorry."

Her words are cryptic and stoke my curiosity.

"Don't ever be. You'll tell when you're ready for my help."

"I'll never—"

Done with her defiance, I shove the textbooks off the bed, shove her back, and then flip her on her stomach. My hands toy with her waistband.

"Seven, what are you doing?" She glances at me over her shoulder. Watches as I slide my finger inside her waistband and caress her skin from hip to hip. Her eyes flutter closed. Long lashes sweep over smooth tan skin. Her lips part.

"Seven."

Fuck, I'm hard.

"Scared?"

"Of you? Never."

Good. I tug at the waistband. "Yes or no, Leigh?"

She drops her head onto the pillow. Her answer is muffled.

"I didn't hear you."

"Yes. Jesus, Seven."

"Lift your hips, baby."

She does. I take off her yoga pants and palm her ass through her Captain America underwear. She trembles. I coast my fingers down her bare legs.

She kicks them up and down and nearly nails me in the family jewels. It'd be worth getting kicked in the balls 'cause when she did the scissor motion with her legs, she gave me a glimpse of how wet she is. Leigh is so wet, her underwear clings to her pussy.

I bite down on my knuckles and groan.

"Crap, did I kick you in the balls?"

"You mean my very *blue* balls?"

Since those corner mouth kisses of ours, all I think about is kissing up and down Leigh's body and having her put her mouth on other parts of me. I would go down on her in a heartbeat. Eat out her pussy for hours if she asked it of me. Her giving me blow? I'll always leave that in her hands. I would never force or pressure a girl for blow, a hand job, or sex.

"Is it that bad?"

"Since our kiss," I admit.

"Should we stop?"

"Hell no!"

Low laughter from her.

"Don't blue balls hurt?"

"I can get off using my hand." The tips of my ears heat. I've never told a girl that. Or admit to one that she gives me blue balls from her kisses alone. Then again, no girl's affected me like Leigh has, including Meisa.

"Don't guys just ask for a BJ from a willing girl? You do have your fair share of them. I doubt any of them would've settled for a dumb kiss on the side of the mouth."

And that there is what sets her apart from the other girls.

"Leigh, I don't want to talk about my junk or other girls." I slide my hand down her leg and touch the faded cut. "Must've hurt backing into the barbed wire fencing."

"Like a mother," she says. "How'd you guess?"

"I spotted it next to the damn tree. I should put an inflatable mattress under my window in case you fall out of the tree after burglarizing my room."

"Doubtful. I never mess up."

"Take that back," I growl.

"Why?"

"Never say never. You should know better."

"Or else what, Seven Shanahan?"

"You'll fall out of the goddamn tree, that's what."

"Stop saving my life and I'll stop 'borrowing' your stuff."

"I'll always save your life, Leigh. There are no ands, ifs, or buts about it."

She rolls onto her back and kicks at me. "Study time. It's the reason you're here, isn't it?"

It is, but I cannot get out of my head Leigh falling out of the tree. Maybe I should talk to Dad about having a security system installed on the house. He's avoided having one put in saying he feels safer without extra eyes and ears on the house. In the meantime, I can call in a tree service and have them cut off the limbs.

Yeah, my dad will love that, coming home to a limbless tree. He'll think I went nutso and will go after his balls next for cheating on my kindhearted mom. *Maybe* cheated. The verdict is still out on that one.

With her body half on, half off the bed, Leigh picks up the books and my notebook off the floor.

"Pull me up." I hear from under her mass of thick hair.

Uh-uh. Not yet. I have a nice view of her ass cheeks poking out from under her underwear. My fingers itch to caress the underside of her tan ass.

"Seven, did you hear me?"

Talking my boner down again, I grab Leigh by the waist and haul her back on the bed.

With my stuff clasped to her chest, she twists her body and faces me. Pink dots her cheeks, and she is breathing heavy. Dumping the stuff on the bed, she pats the spot in front of her. I have a better idea.

I tuck my hands under her arms and settle her between my outstretched legs. With my back resting on the wall, I nuzzle the curve of her neck and point at the textbooks.

"I'm failing history and leadership. But you already know that."

"History will be easy. Leadership is something else. You haven't turned in what's sinking your grade, a project idea that for phase two, you'll need to put into action."

"What's yours?" I ask.

"I'm not in leadership. My elective is pottery."

"Like making bowls or a giant heart with your handprint in the middle?"

My smartass comment gets me low laughter from her.

"What's wrong with my hand on a giant heart?"

"Nothing. Nothing at all," I say into her hair, the strands soft. She also smells good. Flowers. Roses and lilacs? My mom has a shit ton of them growing in the back of the house. A place that is an explosion of reds, purples, whites, and yellows from spring to late summer. Mom says her flower garden is her sanctuary.

"Leigh, can I ask a personal question about your parents?"

"I thought we were studying?"

"If you don't want to get personal—"

"Ask away, Seven. I like talking about my parents."

She misses them, and I'm a bastard for being angry with my parents for their mess of a marriage. Why'd Dad have to get caught with someone who is not my mom in his hotel room?

Has Leigh heard from her friend, the one she stole a three-mil car from? Shit, we have a ton to talk about. I've never had so much to talk about with a girl before. It's weird. A turn on too.

"You said your parents were very in love. Is it because they had date nights? Went on trips all the time? He brought her flowers and chocolates? Went out of his way to do romantic shit for her?"

"They didn't do much of date nights or taking trips."

She plays with my pant leg. Grabs and tugs at the denim.

"We didn't have a lot of money. My dad brought home flowers from the restaurants he worked at. He took them off the tables when he closed. The owners liked my dad and gave him the okay. Romance is them reminiscing about the day they met and those first few weeks of falling madly in love."

She reaches behind, cradles the back of my head, and tips her face to mine.

"It's how they stayed in love. They talked all the time. Sometimes into the early hours of morning. They were each other's best friends."

"That's sweet, Leigh. Thank you for telling me. Your parents sound cool. I would've loved to meet them were they alive." Honest-to-God truth.

"They'd like you."

"Really?"

"Well, yeah, 'cause I find you so utterly annoying." She rubs her nose on the underside of my jaw and presses her mouth on my skin. "You are. So. Much. So."

Her soft lips on my skin. Her warm breath. Her sweet scent. *Fuck.*

"*Leigh.*"

"Hmm?"

"You're equally annoying," I say. Anything to calm my junk. I'm ready to jizz in my pants, and I haven't done much except smell her and feel her mouth on my jaw. My jaw, for fuck's sake.

"We're agreeing again. That's not good. We're supposed to be enemies. Tell me something I'd hate you for."

"You have pussy dimples?"

She laughs. "What the hell are those? And no way do I have them."

"Shall we look?"

"We shall not. Jesus, Seven."

She's still laughing. I curve my arms around her and pull her all the way against me. It's amazing how well we fit. I rest my chin on the top of her head.

"Did that guy you stole the Bugatti from get ahold of you?"

"Not yet."

Her cell on the nightstand buzzes. She moves from between my legs and hops off the bed. Leigh brings the screen to her face.

"Speak of the devil. God, I hope he didn't bug the place." Her gaze shoots around her room. "I wouldn't put it past him." She answers the call and puts the phone on the nightstand. "You're on speaker so don't say anything inappropriate or something that will have me hunting you down."

"Like you could, kiddo, and I'll say any goddamn

inappropriate thing I'd like."

"Nice to hear your asshatedness, again, M."

"M?" I mouth.

She bites down on her bottom lip, looking sexy as fuck. I want to grab the phone from her, end the call, and kiss her breathless.

Deep chuckle from the other end of the line. "What's up, Leigh?"

"I'm calling in a favor."

"Sorry, kid, but you're in my debt and not the other way around."

"We're even, M." She paces with her hands on her hips and a deep furrow between her brows. Leigh is concocting a plan. I perk up. Get a stiffy too. I mean, come on, she's got brains and looks.

"How's that?"

"I might've *borrowed* something of yours before I left Cali."

"What did you *steal*, little one?"

"Borrowed."

"Semantics," he growls. "Fess up, Leigh!"

"Where are you calling me from?"

"My penthouse."

"The one in San Francisco?"

"Yeah."

"How many are there?" I say in a low voice.

She flashes her fingers on both hands, then holds up two fingers. Holy fuck. This dude has *twelve* penthouses?

"Okay, go to your master bedroom closet. The one on the right side of your bed."

She was *inside* his bedroom? I rise off the bed and march for the phone. Her palm jams against my chest. I knock aside her hand and glower. She rolls her eyes and points at the bed, mouthing for me to sit my ass down.

Defiant, bossy, *and* evasive. I return to my old spot on the bed and grouse. Fuck's sake, why won't she let me ream out the rich dude for showing *a minor* his stinking bedroom? Leigh didn't become an "adult" until a month ago.

There's silence on the other end, followed by the noise of a door sliding on tracks.

"Are you there yet?"

"Yeah."

"Is something missing from the top shelf?"

A pregnant pause. Then all hell breaks loose.

"What the fuck? Where are my tapes? I'm coming for you, Leigh."

Over my dead body will the dude hurt her.

"Don't worry, your sex tapes are safe."

"How safe? Those are A-list celebrities I fucked. I

signed *NDAs*."

Non-disclosure agreements. How do I know what that shit acronym means? My dad's high-profile clients have him sign one before he takes on a job. He gave me a glimpse into his world when I overheard him speaking to my uncle about it years ago.

"Under the ground safe. In a fireproof safe."

She tips her head behind her. No way did she bury his sex tapes behind the guesthouse. As though she read my mind, she nods. Remind me not to mess with her. Or make a sex tape. Or sign an NDA.

"Will you help now?"

"Go ahead, ask. But, Leigh, after I do this favor and you return the tapes, there will be hell to pay. If you thought three months in juvie was a walk in the park, what I have planned for you is nothing short of a monster wedgie."

Her eyes widen. She shoves her fist against her mouth. Too late. Laughter bursts from her, and that's how I know this Maddox dude is cool and can be counted on to do right by Leigh. He loves the hell out of my best friend girl.

Rewind. We are not friends. Leigh and I will never be just friends. I gave her my word, and I'm good for it.

22

For the rest of the week, Seven and I fall into a routine. At school, he picks on me every chance he gets, which isn't often. I learned his habits and avoid running into him and his friends and teammates.

At night, around midnight, he'll come into my bedroom through the window. We talk about everything under the sun. Go over the good and the bad of our day too. It's nice having someone to talk to. Nice having an "enemy" who only wants to "never be just friends," whatever that means.

I'm scared to ask Seven. Something more is happening with us, and I don't want to ruin this weird rhythm of us hating-to-love and loving-to-hate one another thing between us.

In other non-Seven news, Thomas texts me every day. We even had a video chat. That was nice too, though I felt like a traitor for laughing at his corny jokes.

But I have a feeling Alistair and my mom are smiling down at me from heaven for giving Thomas the chance to be a father to me. Henry and I text daily too. His messages are along the lines of "how is your day?" and "make any friends?" My favorite is, "any guy giving you a hard time? Let me know and I'll kick his ass."

I don't know what to think of Henry's sudden overprotectiveness other than one—he's kissing up, desperate for someone to keep an eye on Hannah and talk sense into her constant partying. She is gone nightly since Thomas and Eleanor left for their trip. Two, he has serious problems at DU and is overcompensating by putting my well-being at the top of his overcompensation list.

Curious, I trolled him and his ex-girlfriend on social media. The redhead is stunning. The guy she cheated on and left Henry for is equally stunning.

The guy is a senior and is on Dumas' football team. He's a jerk too. There is a video of him taunting Henry, calling him a loser. Henry didn't make the cut for the football team.

Henry doesn't take well to the public shaming. He throws a punch. The jerk sidesteps him and throws his own punch, knocking Henry on his ass. Henry's face swells up, and he staggers to his feet. He goes for round two, but his friends hold him back and haul him out of the view of the camera. I recognize the guys with him. They were with Henry the night he tried drowning me in the pool.

Fuming, I call Rue. She answers right away.

"What's up?"

"Got plans this Saturday? If not, let's go on a road trip."

"Where?"

"Dumas."

"Aren't you working at Queenie's?"

"I have this Saturday off."

"Why Dumas?"

I run my plan by her. "Is two days enough time to get everything set up? Can we stay with your sister?"

"I can do you one better, but Red will have to come with."

I like Red, so it's not a problem that he tags along. "The more the merrier. Thanks, Rue, I appreciate it."

On the day of the party, I sit out on the bleachers and watch the football team practice. The same jerk gives me a hard time. As we agreed on when he dropped me off, Malice takes back his word in front of a crowd during lunch period. He and I are not an item. He was toying with me and his teammates. A joke, that's all.

I don't miss the triumphant gleam in Seven's dark eyes, followed by him clenching his jaw when the jerk cackles and loudly says, "Jinx. I knew you were playing us, bro. Who wants to date her anyway? She's fucking weird."

That was Tuesday. I stayed for practice and made it on the activity bus right as the doors closed. Someone must have told the driver to wait for me. Yesterday was the same old story, with me sticking around at Seven's practice and then studying at my place. Seven came over with sweet treats for me and protein-loaded snacks for him. We snacked and studied. When dinnertime rolled around, we took turns picking what we ate.

Monday was pizza. Tuesday, teriyaki. Yesterday, burgers. He didn't mention Malice or his jerk teammate. We talked about the first thing that came to our minds. Yesterday, it was our ideal pets.

Mine is a big dog. Him, too, the meaner the better, but a softie at heart. Why doesn't that surprise me? Seven wants a dog that reflects who he is. I told him he should get a pug. I hear they snore.

For my comment, he got me on the couch and tickled me. Wanting to get back at him, I stuck my hand down his mesh shorts and pinched his ass cheek. I expected a yelp but not the deep groan reverberating against my chest.

Turned on by him being turned on, my hands slid to the front of his shorts, and more forward than I've been with him, I touched his erection, my fingers gliding over his thickness and the velvety tip of his penis. He hid his groan in my neck, and out of breath with need, I stopped touching him. He pulled me on top of him, out of breath too, and we stayed like that until he softened and our breathing returned to normal.

Being with Seven has me wanting to give him my everything. My dreams. My doubts. My heartaches. My failures. My defiance. My *body*.

The wind and rain pick up, and I hunch forward and draw my shoulders inward. The last three days has been this annoying drizzle that covers my face like a spray bottle on "mist" setting. It also obscures my sight. I would rather have the skies open and dump rain than put up with "the mist."

My wish came true. It is dumping, and my umbrella is bearing the brunt of the fat drops pounding on it. Holding on to the handle with one hand, I shove my other hand in my jacket pocket. My teeth chatter. I cocoon my backpack between my feet. With my luck, it'll fall in the gap in the bleachers and I'll have to go after it.

In my line of sight, I see a pair of cleats coming closer to me. I slide my eyes upward. Seven is running toward me.

"Hey, wait for me inside my truck. Make sure you turn on the heat. I can hear your teeth chattering from across the field."

I tip the umbrella back so I can see him. He is soaking wet, and drops of rain cling to his skin, his long lashes, and his mouth. I want to flick the tip of my tongue on all those places and lick at the drops. His skin would be cool. Salty too.

"Don't stare at me like that, Leigh." He blinks at the raindrops in his eyes. "Go before I do something we'll regret."

What could he be regretting? It can't be the temptation to kiss me. We've kissed many times, with and without tongues, and he's never said he regretted kissing me. In fact, he asked if he could keep on kissing me.

"The guys will think something's going on between us."

"Well, yeah. I told them you're out here freezing

your ass off because you're helping me pass my classes."

"You did?"

He cups the back of his neck. "It's my own damn fault you're out here in the cold and rain. It's time I take responsibility for my fuck-ups." He hands me his truck keys.

I am so proud of him for owning his mistakes, I don't defy. Or think too hard on how he hasn't told his friends and teammates we're more than study buddies. I take the keys from him.

"Thank you, Seven. I'll see you soon."

Does he agree with his jerk teammate that I'm weird and he wouldn't date me? Is Seven embarrassed or ashamed to be seen in public with me as anything more than his tutor? Is he that concerned with what everyone thinks of him? Is he interested in Ginger? I wouldn't blame him if he is. She's drop dead gorgeous, has great fashion sense, is liked by everyone, and she doesn't rock the boat. Compared to me, Ginger is an angel.

Why go down the road paved with doubt? If I do, I'll have to give up spending time with Seven. Put the screen back on over my bedroom window. Keep him out of my life, my mind, and my heart.

"Soon. Get warm quick, yeah?"

"Yep."

He helps me down from the bleachers, one hand holding the umbrella over my head and the other holding my free hand. After my feet are firmly on the ground and he hands me back the umbrella, Seven runs over to his teammates.

Malice and Trace high-five him. His coach clamps his hand on Seven's shoulder and squeezes. They exchange words. Seven glances my way with a smile on his face. Our gazes lock, and he gives me a two-finger salute.

My heart pitter-patters as hard as the rain pounding the ground around me. For the rest of practice, I divide my time watching Seven and wondering how I'll invite myself to the party Hannah's going to tonight.

I don't have to wonder long. I get a text from Rue. There's this happening party tonight. The guy hosting it goes to her school, and the girl he's dating goes to mine. How perfect is that? "Very," I text back, smiling. She is a social butterfly and doesn't let school rivalries get in the way of having fun.

I read her next text.

Rue: Bonus? Shay and Winslow will be there. They're good guys

Me: I am in. See you later

I hold my cell to my chest, excited for my first party since moving to Cambridge. Too bad Seven won't be there. He told me yesterday he won't be coming over tonight. There is a huge quiz tomorrow in his finance class, and he'll be up late studying. That guy is on the right track.

I look up. Practice is over, and he's sauntering over to the truck. I check him out from head to toe. His dark hair is plastered to his head, and his uniform molds to his body. He is all bulk with the padding he's wearing under the uniform, but he moves with the grace and stealth of a predator on the hunt.

The intense way he looks at me tells me I am the prey. Heat uncoils in my core and pools in my girl parts. Seven is downright sexy, but it's not his good looks that draws me to him, though it's a bonus.

What has me falling hard is how kind he is, and he hides this kindness well, using his bad-boy jerk image to his advantage. It's brilliant, but I won't be telling him I'm onto him anytime soon.

There's a good chance he'll stop doing good just to prove to me how bad he is. Reverse psychology. I shake my head. That boy.

He pays more than the asking price for the items that the poorer kids at our school are selling on this buy, sell app. If that kid dares inflate the price for someone other than Seven, Seven will give the kid a bad rating *and* make his life at and outside school miserable. That's what I overheard as he paced outside my front door, haggling a higher price with the seller. Who does that? Um, apparently Seven Shanahan.

Seven also pays another kid good money to detail his truck and wash it spotless. Who does that when it's been raining off and on, and has the kid seen Seven's cleats after practice? They are *filthy*.

"Warm enough?"

"Yes, thanks."

"Ready to go?"

I nod.

"Good, 'cause I'm taking a shower at your place. Afterward, I plan on kissing you for being so agreeable."

If his kisses are my reward, I should be more agreeable. Except kissing Seven won't be enough. I'll want more.

With how uncertain my future is, there's not room for more, so why wish for it? Why set myself up for disappointment?

23

---

*R*ue doesn't pick me up until after nine.

"It's better to be late than on time," she says as soon as I get inside her car.

"I'm not a partier, so whatever works." I buckle. "I thought Red would be riding with us."

"He'll meet us there." She pulls away from the fence and gets back on the road.

"And these guys you want me to meet?"

"They won't show up until closer to ten."

"The party runs that late on a school night?"

"Yep. There's no rest for the wicked or the rich. By the way, I love your outfit. You're rocking the badass look."

"Thanks."

That was my intention, to come off as don't mess

with me or I'll mess with you, in case one or both of the pervy brothers go after Hannah. Except now that I'm sitting, I am having second thoughts on my choice of clothes, a short spaghetti-strap leopard print dress pulled over a long-sleeved black shirt paired with black combat boots.

It doesn't take long to get to the party house. By the looks of it, the party is in full swing. There are cars lined up and down both sides of the road.

Rue parks at the bottom of the street—one of the few spots left—and we walk up the road to the house at the top of the hill. The music is loud, a rap song. There's whooping and hollering from a bunch of guys, followed by girls laughing and shouting their encouragement.

"Drink, drink, drink!"

"Is there underage drinking going on?" I ask.

"You betcha."

"I take it there are no adults around?"

"None." She clucks her tongue. "Get used to it. The parents out here are either helicopter parents or they parent from a distance from wherever they're making their money from."

"Which category do you fall into?"

Silence. Then it hits me.

"I'm sorry, Rue. It was insensitive of me to ask. I

mean, I don't know anything about your life." Are her parents together? Divorced? Is one of them dead and the other alive? Remarried?

"Don't be sorry. If I don't want you to know, I'll tell, okay?"

"Thanks, Rue."

She's a good person. My first real friend who's a girl.

"I have no clue where my mom is."

She crosses her arms over her chest, and we walk up the street side by side, her in her wedge heels and me in my combat boots.

"I never knew my father. He left before I was born. Good news? Me and Riley have the same father."

Unlike Riley's friend Arie, whose siblings have different fathers.

Thankful she shared, I reciprocate. "I didn't find out the man who raised me, who I thought was my father, wasn't until the day he died. He told me I wasn't his biological daughter. My mom never said a word."

"Aw, I'm so sorry, Leigh." She stops and pulls me in for a hug. "Family can be messed up, right?"

"Isn't that the truth?"

She lets me go and nods at the huge house nestled in the woods. "Ready to party?"

I glance at the house with the wall of windows and the wraparound deck. Kids are dancing, drinking, laughing. Things I want to do. First, I have to find Hannah. I let Rue tug me to the house. The majority of the kids are from Delridge. I recognize a handful from Cambridge. They stare but don't acknowledge me.

Rue sticks close by my side, but I can tell she is antsy and wants to hang out with her friends. The group of girls is by the table of food, talking. On a chair on the other side of the table, next to a tall, willowy blonde in a pretty fuchsia red dress, is a small laundry hamper that is more tall than wide. Rue looks where I'm looking.

"That's where they're keeping the prize money for whoever wins the scavenger hunt. You have to put in fifty dollars, and they'll give you a ticket."

Henry didn't mention that part to me.

"Crap. I didn't bring cash."

"I did. I'll buy your ticket."

"Thanks, Rue. If I win, I'll split the winnings fifty-fifty."

"No need. Just give me back the fifty."

"Are you sure?"

"Yes. I'm glad you came with."

So am I. Being here is a change from the loneliness I feel when I am in my place. The silence is deafening without Seven's presence filling up the space.

"Hey, I'm going to get a drink."

"Want me to go with?"

"I'll be fine. Go talk to your friends." I tip my chin at the girls by the table.

"I should introduce you—"

"Go. Be gone." I give her a gentle push toward her friends. "I'll text you if I need a babysitter."

"I'm your bodyguard."

"Or a cockblocker in disguise."

"Anything but that. Text me if you need help out of a bind." Phone in hand, she waves.

I blow out a quiet breath. Finally. I can go look for Hannah, but I feel bad that I didn't go with Rue and meet her friends.

Vowing that I'll ask her for an introduction later, I hurry inside the house. My across-the-shoulder small bag whaps my hip. No matter where I go, I keep my EpiPen and my cell with me.

I go in through the sliding glass door and find myself in the kitchen. There's a guy next to the fridge. He's older, probably in his early to mid-twenties, with reddish hair and bright-blue eyes. In his hand is a red plastic cup. In the other is an e-cigarette. He takes a long drag, then blows out smoke.

"Party's out there. There's no need to come inside unless there's something other than food and beer you're after." His gaze roves over my body.

"The bathroom," I say, staring back at him.

A hint of a smile pulls at the corners of his mouth. "What's your name? Never seen you at one of these shindigs."

There's no harm in giving him my name.

"Nice to meet you, Leigh. Name's Austin."

I assume he's one of the brothers. Where is the other one?

"You go to Delridge?"

"Cambridge. Where's the bathroom?" I need to find Hannah. She's here. I caught a glimpse of her coming up the road before she disappeared inside the house.

"Third door to your right. Don't wander up the stairs, yeah?"

"Not my house, so sure." Um, *of course* I'm heading upstairs. "Thank you!" I give him a small wave and hurry off to the bathroom.

On my way to the "bathroom," I glance over my shoulder. The guy is nowhere in sight.

My heart beating fast, I dart up the stairs and hear voices coming from a room at the end of the hall.

One voice I recognize. Who is the guy with Hannah? I inch closer to the door. They're not quiet.

"Don't do that, please."

"I can do whatever the fuck I want."

The guy is angry. Hannah is . . . Her words are desperate. Similar to the girl who was almost raped by one of my foster brothers.

I absently reach for the aluminum bat poking from the dumpster and grab air. Crap! I only have my bag and my fists. I left the mace and switchblade on top of my dresser. Balling my hands, I press my ear to the door. Silence. Mattress squeaking.

No. No!

I shove open the door. He is on top of her, holding her arms above her head with his thick fingers tight on her wrists. I see red. A growl rumbles from me. I charge him and jump on his back. My fists slam into the sides of his head.

"Ow. Fuck. What the fuck are you doing?"

He rears backward. I clamp my arms and legs

around him. He tries bucking me off. I hold on for dear life.

"Hurt her again and I'll kick you in the balls," I hiss.

He grabs at my fingers and tries prying them from around his neck. I interlock them. He gags. I'm choking him and should let go. I can't. He hurt Hannah.

Small arms wrap around my waist from behind, and a soft voice says next to my ear, "Leigh, that's my boyfriend you're trying to murder."

Boyfriend? I let go. He rocks forward, grabbing at his throat. Starts having a coughing fit. I pound on his back. He swats at my hand. I tip back, knocking Hannah over. I roll off her and the bed and get on my feet.

"I'm so sorry," I tell the boyfriend before saying to Hannah, "I thought you were interested in someone else."

She looks confused, and then her eyes widen. "You mean Seven?"

I nod.

"I did it to save you from him. He has a one-track mind and can be an ass when something doesn't go his way or someone stops him from having what he wants. Cam knows I've been flirting with the jerk in order to steer him away from you."

"Cool, isn't she? Full disclosure. Doesn't hold back. Too bad she wants to keep our relationship a secret."

It's not a well-kept one if Henry called me specifically asking I keep an eye on Hannah.

"So the mean girl attitude—"

"Was an act. I thought you would drop from his radar that first day he picked on you, but you didn't. I'm sorry, Leigh."

"It's okay. Thank you for helping me. Seven is a pain in the ass."

"I second that."

She smiles. I smile back.

"You and an older guy, huh?"

"Love at first sight." She slides her arm across Cam's shoulders. They're sitting on the bed, resting against the headboard. "Will you tell Henry?"

"Not my secret. So all those parties you've been going to while your parents are gone is to come here?"

"Yes." She plants a kiss on Cam's hair.

"Henry said Brody's older brothers are perverts who like the girls young. If they're not pedophiles or weirdos, why not tell Henry? He was worried."

"I'm sorry he misled you. He has good intentions. Thinks Cam will hurt me the way Ashley hurt him."

"I don't understand."

She bites down on her bottom lip. "Leigh, Henry's ex is Cam's younger sister."

Everything falls into place. "Awkward."

"It is. Can you see why he wouldn't like me and Cam to be together? That's the reason you're here, isn't it, to report back to him what you find?"

"I'm not a snitch."

"I can trust you?"

"Hannah, I'm not a pawn to be played by you and Henry."

Keeping her secret reminds me of what I did for my mother. What I'm doing for Sorrow. Nothing ends well where secrets are involved.

"We should tell him, babe." Cam takes her hand and kisses her knuckles. "My sis can be a real bitch, and I don't want her representing the family. We're better people than that, tossing someone away when they're not useful any longer."

What does he mean by that? It doesn't look like Henry's ex used him for money. This place must've cost a fortune.

"I said I don't want you to tell. Not yet, Cam.

Give Henry time to get over Ashley, and then we'll get him used to us."

Was that what they were talking about? What I misconstrued as him forcing himself on her, doing whatever the eff he wants? I walk backward until I'm at the door.

"I should go and give you two privacy. Again, I'm sorry for attacking you."

"Nah, no worries. Hannah told me about you. You're cool having her back like that, coming to her rescue with those mean-as-fuck fists of yours. Nice to meet you, Leigh."

"You too, Cam."

I leave them be, relieved there wasn't a baseball bat nearby. Or mace and a switchblade in my hands. Needing space and a quiet place to collect myself, I walk past groups of kids dancing to rap music and drinking from red cups.

The perfect spot presents itself. A bench on the back side of a wooden shed. I sit, and closing my eyes, I rest back against the shed.

Poor Henry. To go off to college with someone you believed loved you, only to be cheated on and dumped for the next best thing.

Is that what Seven will do when I stop defying him? He'll lose interest and move on to the next target? Or he'll realize I'm not good enough, will never belong in his world of money, and ditch me for someone who does?

Then I hear it. Seven's voice in my head. "Leigh, in this, can you just be and enjoy what you have in the here and now?"

I smile. How did that boy get so wise?

I pull my knee up to my chest and listen to the crickets and the frogs. Voices cut into my solitude and the delicious memory of Seven singing as he showered at my place after practice today.

Tomorrow, the team will be at an away game. Seven said he'll be too tired to pay me a midnight visit. Good. I'd like to go hang out with Sorrow. Her dad should be passed out drunk. She said he usually is after dinner.

"Shay, why are you taking me away from the party?"

"To show you a magic trick."

I roll my eyes. The guy with the "magic trick" is Rue's friend Shay?

"That's the dumbest pickup line."

"It's not a line."

Poor guy, she completely plows past his growl of frustration.

"Why do you think you have a chance with me, anyway? Why would I go out with a guy who has a girl's name?"

"It's a unisex name, means hawk, and because my parents are fucking Irish."

I can picture him jamming his fingers through his hair. Not wanting to get called out for eavesdropping—hello, I was here first—I rise and walk from behind the shed.

She's gone, and he has his hands crammed in his pants pockets.

"Good riddance. She didn't deserve you."

"That so?" He pulls his shoulders to his core and looks me up and down, his gaze stuck on my boots. "What's with the hardcore footwear?"

"In case I need to kick some girl's ass for turning down a boy's magic show."

He laughs. "Gotcha."

"I'd love for you to show me your magic trick."

"Really? You don't think it's a dumb line?"

"Why? Was it a trick to get her to come over here with you?"

"I can get a girl to do whatever the hell I want without resorting to tricks."

"Um, excuse me, but I just watched your ego crash and burn."

"Not my fault she's the new girl and doesn't know when to bow to the king on campus."

Wow, he is full of himself. Reminds me of another full-of-himself king on campus.

"Show me your trick." Worst case, he doesn't have one. Best case? I make a new friend. Shay can't be that bad of a guy if he is friends with Rue.

"Cool. You won't regret it."

"You won't either unless you try to stick your hands or your tongue anywhere on my body."

He smiles big. "Noted. Okay, do you have two quarters?"

"Why would I bring change to a party?"

"Good point. That's why I brought my own."

I bite down on my smile. Rue's friend is awesome.

He takes his hands out of his pockets and opens one of his palms. He's holding two quarters.

"What do you see?"

"Two quarters."

"Good. That's good. Ready?"

"For what?"

"The magic."

I stifle my laughter with my hand. He is giddy with excitement. "Um, sure?"

"Watch closely." He moves the quarters from one hand to the other. First, slowly, then he picks up speed. How he doesn't drop the coins is beyond me. I watch, my eyes narrowed, trying to keep up with his movements. Finally, he stops with his hands balled.

He nods at the tops of his hands. "Which hand is holding the quarters?"

I tap his right. He turns his hand and opens his palm. Empty. He shows me his other hand. Also empty. I look at the ground in case he dropped the coins. The lights mounted on the sides of the shed shine on dirt.

Okay, then.

"Where'd they go?"

"Hmm, let me take a gander."

A gander? Who talks like this? Laughing, I shake my head.

"Hold still." He steps into my personal space, and leaning into me, he slides his hand across my shoulder and under my hair.

"Hey, what are you doing?" I lift my knee then stop. Rue wouldn't be friends with a guy who takes advantage of a girl by showing her his "magic trick."

"Taking a gander for the coins."

"Down my collar?"

"In your fine-ass hair," he says near my ear.

His fingers are firmly trenched in my hair when a large shadow falls on us. In my peripheral vision, Seven is stomping toward us. Trace and Malice fall in line behind him. He is smoking hot in a black shirt and low-hung jeans. I have the strong urge to run over, get him behind a tree, and stick my hands under his shirt and down his pants. He would be solid and warm.

But why is Seven here instead of at home studying? I twist around and spot Ginger in the crowd. Was him studying an excuse to come to a party he didn't think I'd be at? Is he here looking for an easy hookup?

"Seven, what are you doing here?"

"I should ask the same of you, Leigh."

"Ah, so you're Leigh."

Seven's attention swivels from me to Shay. "What the fuck does that mean? And let the fuck go of her hair, douchebag."

"Or else what?"

"I'll fuck up your face, that's what."

"Leigh, does this guy mean something to you?" Shay tugs me back against him with his hand on my hip. The way he says the words, his hold on me . . . It speaks of this *thing* between us.

Seven steps forward with his fists clenched at his sides and his jaw locked. This will not end well for Rue's friend, and I don't want to mess up our friendship before it's begun.

"Shay, do as he says."

"You know this fucker's name?" His attention lands back on my face.

"Seven, *please*."

"What did I tell you about begging, Leigh?"

I tip my chin. "This isn't what you think. Shay's showing me a magic trick. He was looking for these disappearing quarters. My hair got caught in his watch's wristband."

It's true. When I tipped my chin at Seven, the metal gripped my hair.

"I don't give a fuck what you were doing with him so long as he lets you go. Now."

He advances with his arm pulled back. Shay shoves me out of the way. His wrist slides out of his watch's metal band. Landing against the shed, I watch in horror as Seven's fist connects with Shay's face again and again.

Shay punches back, but Seven is quick. He dodges the blows, and with his head down, he plows into Shay's stomach. The two fall onto the ground.

"Do something!" I tell Malice.

Malice blinks out of whatever trance he's in and yanks Seven off Shay. I hurry to Shay, and on my hands and knees, I apologize over and over.

"He didn't mean to. I'm so sorry."

His face is swollen, and his lip is split.

"Help me up."

I slide my arm under his shoulders and gently prop him up. "Please don't press charges," I say near his ear. "I'll do anything."

"Anything?"

"Yes." If Seven is charged for assault, he won't be able to play for the rest of the season.

"He's into you. Why?"

"He hates me."

"Then he'll hate you more for going to homecoming with the rival school's quarterback."

Shay plays for the Daredevils? Is he the football player Seven hates, the one Allison cheated on him with? But he told me it was a Sterling who raped Allison. Except Red never talked football. Unless it's a different Sterling boy. Seven said they're a huge family. Gah! I am so confused.

"Are you by chance a Sterling?"

"Other than Malice here, I'm it, Leigh."

I look in the direction of the familiar voice. "Red?"

"Wait, you know this fucker too?" Seven's glower swings from me and Shay to Red and Rue.

I help Shay stand. No use sitting on our asses. It's a weak position to be in when there's a predator nearby.

"Red saved me from being roadkill."

Seven looks from Red to me. His eyes widen, having put two and two together.

"You *owe* him?"

Before I can say a word, Red puts in his two cents. "She does, and I intend on collecting. Tonight. In one of the bedrooms. Unless Leigh would rather owe me in the back of my Escalade."

"*Red*." I plead with my eyes for him to stop with the taunting. Has he looked at Shay's face?

Seven storms over, grabs my arm, and pulls me away from the group, out of earshot.

"Tell me you evened the score and stole something of his?"

"Why would I do that?"

"Because you did it to me. You're not in the business of owing anyone, remember?"

"Of course I do. I'm the one who said those words." I yank my arm out of his grip. "I only steal for leverage or because I care."

He narrows his eyes. "Which is it with me?"

"Both, okay?"

"Time to pay up, Leigh," Red says with too much satisfaction in his voice.

Damn him. I am going to tear into him for taunting Seven. I march over to give him a piece of my mind. Rough hands grab me by the waist and yank me back against a solid body.

"You're not going anywhere with that bastard. He hurt Allison."

"What the hell did you accuse me of?"

"You heard me."

A crowd is gathering. Red tips his head. "You believe him, Leigh?"

"I don't know what to believe, but Seven believes Allison."

Red glares at Seven. "You think I dicked around with your girlfriend at that damn party?"

"That's what she said, and she is not my girl. Not anymore."

Red shakes his head. "Dude, get your head on straight. She's playing you. Come on, Leigh. Time to pay up."

He extends his hand to me. Is Red right and Allison is messing with Seven's head with her accusation of rape? I'm not clueless she still has feelings for him.

Why would a girl lie about something as serious as rape? But that girl my foster brother almost raped protected him and turned me in to the cops for breaking his arm. People do strange things in the name of love.

I take a step toward Red, ready for resistance from Seven. Imagine my disappointment when he lets me go. Setting my hand in Red's, I reach for Shay

"Come on, big guy. Let's get ice on your face and hands."

He comes over, and not paying Seven any attention, he reaches under my hair and untangles the watch from the strands. Shay slides the Rolex over his wrist. Seven wedges his body between me and Shay.

"What am I, chop liver?" He shows me his hands, fingertips pointing at the ground. His knuckles are swollen.

I angle my head back toward the crowd. "I'm sure Ginger is more than willing to help you with that."

I don't give him the chance to stop me or say something stupid, like make excuses for his presence here. He came to the party to hook up with her, I'm certain of it.

Red tugs me behind him to the house, bringing me out of my thoughts. Shay and Rue follow us. They're talking in low voices. I hope this isn't the end of our friendship. As we get closer to the house, the path widens. Red yanks me forward, then clasps me against his side. We walk hip to hip up the path.

Inside the house, he leads me upstairs and to one of the bedrooms. Rue and Shay hang back in the kitchen. Cam's brother sees Shay's face. A whistle edges out from between his teeth.

"Need a pack of peas?"

"Yeah, thanks."

The conversation drifts to us just before Red closes the bedroom door. I back up until my legs hit the bedframe.

"Red, why are we here?"

"I'm testing a hunch. One." He takes a step. "Two." Another step. "Three."

The door crashes open, and Seven barges in. I expect him to throw a punch. What I'm not expecting is the tight control he has over his body. His body is pulled taut. One move from Red and Seven will be on top of him, fists flying.

"What game are you playing at, Sterling?"

"The game of who gets her first. I saved your girl's life. She owes me."

"You're wrong. She's my property, so it'll be me who owes you."

I am his *property*?

"Name your price and I'll give. Then we'll call ourselves even."

"Anything?"

"Anything."

"What if I want a night with her?"

"Hey, I'm right here." I wedge between them and glare.

Seven moves me off to the side with his hands on my shoulders.

"Not in the cards. Ask for something else."

"You sure about that? It'd be easy to walk out that door and forget her."

"I'm sure."

"Last chance, Shanahan. There's plenty of pussy out there waiting for you."

"I said I'm sure. What do you want, Sterling?"

Ruthless gleam in Red's eyes. "Your lucky coin. Hand it over."

25

LEIGH

*A*fter Seven handed his lucky coin over to Red, he left the room, not even sparing me a backward glance.

He did what he came into the room for. He evened the score. I don't owe Red anymore. That doesn't mean I'm less pissed at either of them. I am not Seven's property or to be used by Red to get back at Seven for the hate that boils between them.

The next day at school, I avoid Seven. At one point, he pulled me into an empty hallway on my way back to class from the restroom. I shook off his hold and demanded he apologize to Shay. Otherwise, he needs to leave me alone. If he doesn't, he'll get a size-six boot shoved up his ass, speaking figuratively.

He'd slammed his palm on the locker and said no way in hell would he apologize. It's beneath him. What a jerk!

"Red, why is there bad blood between you and Seven?" I scoot forward in my seat. Red is driving us to Dumas, and Rue is riding shotgun. Though I've only known Red for a short time, I believe him. That he didn't hurt Allison. Otherwise, his ass wouldn't be on this trip with us.

"You still pissed at me?"

"I am."

"For messing with you, right?"

"Messing with the both of us. You made the situation worse rather than better. If you were wrong, he would always believe something happened between us."

"Don't you want him to?"

"I don't like misleading people."

"He messed with me, Leigh. Misled this girl into thinking I didn't like her when I did. Misled her into believing I slept with her best friend. That's the kind of stand-up dude you're falling for."

I sit back and cross my arms. "I'm not falling for Seven."

"Sure looked like jealousy I saw on your face when you said Ginger's name."

"That's my resting bitch face."

He scoffs. "I saw what I saw, Leigh. Drop it already."

"What will it take to make things right between you two?"

"When my team kicks his team's ass at the homecoming game."

Shit. I agreed on going to that game and the homecoming dance with Shay the following night.

"Where's the girl now?" I ask. Anything to distract me from my agreement with Seven's rival.

"She moved away when I was away at camp. I never got to tell her the truth."

No wonder he's mad. "I'm sorry."

"Let the fucker go, Leigh. There are other guys. Guys with heart."

"Like Shay?"

"Shay's hung up on a girl. Winslow isn't."

"Did he catch feelings for the new girl?"

"Nah, he was making the girl he wants jealous."

"One of my friends," Rue says. "Blair. Tall, pretty blonde standing next to the table of drinks and food."

I remember her.

"She's super shy. Shay was hoping she'd fight this new girl for his attention."

I roll my eyes. "There is something wrong with all of you."

"Welcome to high school drama." Rue shoots a toothy grin at me over her shoulder. "We're almost to Dumas. Are you excited?"

"I'd be more excited if we were staying with your sister instead of with Midnight."

"But he is so hot. And Dare? He's smoking hot."

"Gross, Rue."

"It's the truth, Red."

"Can it, okay? I don't need to know my best friend girl is wet for my brother and my cousin. Make sure you don't stay in a room with Dare for too long, Leigh. He's *persuasive*."

"Persuasive good? Or persuasive bad?" I ask, my face warm. Seven can be persuasive. Like take off my yoga pants and kiss on my scars persuasive.

"What does that mean?" Red volleys back.

"Both," Rue says. "He'll charm your socks off, then use your socks to jack off in to."

She laughs. I shake my head. Boys.

On the last leg of the drive, I send a text message to Thomas and Hannah that I'm spending the night at a friend's house. They send back a thumbs-up emoji. Wouldn't want Thomas worried when he and

Eleanor arrive home from their vacation this evening.

Soon, Red is parking the SUV in front of a two-story house. Midnight and Dare don't go to Dumas University. Rue said the moment Riley moved to Dumas, Midnight followed. Dare, bored without his wingman and best friend, followed. Midnight bought this house and a block of businesses on the border of Dumas.

We get out of the SUV. We're only staying one night, but when there's a rocking party to go to and a cheating bitch to take down, my friends and I pack for an epic trip of a lifetime.

Red hits a button on the key fob, and the back window rolls down. He walks around, grabs our luggage, and hits the button again. The SUV beeps, and the back window goes up. Rue and I follow him up the brick steps and to the front of the door painted black.

"Is black his favorite color?"

"It's his signature color, yeah. Goes with his name."

"Does that mean yours is red?"

"Nah, mine's blue."

"For the color of your eyes?"

"You got that right, baby." He gives me a sly grin over his shoulder.

I roll my eyes.

Red rings the doorbell. Silence. Then we hear it.

"Get the fucking door, Dare."

"You do it, moron. He's your brother."

"Your cousin, bro."

Rue's laughing into her hand. I smile. "How old did you say they are again?"

"Twenty-three."

"Very mature," I say.

"Hey, go easy on them. They got dropped on their heads by my mom and my aunt."

The door swings open, and had Rue not smacked me across the shoulder, my jaw would've dropped all the way to the ground. Instead, I pick it up off my chest. To say the guy standing on the other side of the door is drop dead gorgeous is an understatement. Spiky jet-ink hair. Deep blue eyes. Dark stubble on a face that would make a saint weep with longing. Tall. Muscular. Tatted. Wearing no shirt. Heather-gray sweatpants hanging low on his hips. Good God, that V-cut. Sculpted some?

"You must be Leigh."

I open my mouth. It's cotton ball dry. I lick my

lips. Try uttering a coherent sentence. "I am. Thanks for offering to help us and on short notice."

"Any friend of Rue's is a friend of mine."

"Stop kissing up, man. She ain't gonna help you get in Riley's good graces."

An equally sexy Adonis steps up to the door, and shoving Midnight aside, he sticks out his hand.

"Dare. Nice to meet you, Leigh."

"You too."

"Come inside our abode. Your bedrooms await you." He rolls his arm and ducks his head.

Midnight pushes him into the door.

"Stop being a dumbass."

I smile. Yep, boys.

For the rest of our time, we go over the plan, then get ready for the party. The party is at this rich guy's place a few blocks from campus. Galley Rutherford is a rugby player known for throwing wild parties. If we can get him and his friends, Xander Brody and Zeke Harrington, to stick with Henry, Henry will be set for the rest of his time at Dumas University.

The girls will love him, and the guys will want to "hang" with him is what Dare promises. Those guys are that popular and have that much sway on and off campus.

"Hey, Leigh, test something for me?"

"What's that?" I rise off the couch, smooth my palm over my red mini dress, and walk over to Dare. He's on the other side of the wet bar.

"There's this thing going around campus. Can two people fall in love if they look into each other's eyes for four minutes?"

"Four minutes is a long time," I say.

"That's a minute of time out hugging times four," Rue says before she pops a potato chip into her mouth.

"I can do the math, Rue."

"Just saying."

"Fine. I can handle four minutes."

"Yes or no?" Dare asks.

"My vote is no, two people cannot fall in love from only looking into each other's eyes."

"Four minutes, Leigh. That's the kicker. We're not talking seconds or a minute. This is two-hundred and forty seconds of intense eye-fucking."

"Eloquent."

Laughing, he points to the barstools on the other side of the wet bar. We sit knee to knee. Red and Rue watch. I rest my arm on the counter, and tipping my head, I meet Dare's gaze. His aqua-colored eyes sparkle. I smile back. Thick fingers skim along my thigh and touch bare skin where the hem of my dress rides up. I smack his hand aside. He smiles and stares back at me. We stay like that for four minutes. Except we do more than look into each other's eyes.

Dare touches my knee, my thigh, my shoulder, and delves his fingers into my hair. I caress his face. Run my knuckles over his coarse stubble. Clutch and squeeze his tatted arms. The sinewy fibers of his muscles dance to my every whim.

When Rue calls time, we sputter laughter.

"Well?"

"Um, no love. You?"

"Totally in love." He moves in for a kiss. I cover my mouth with my palm. His lips kiss the top of my hand. I shove him away with my free hand.

I uncover my mouth. "You're such a flirt."

"Can't say I didn't try. Anyway, I'm prepping you for what's coming later tonight. Looking as hot as you do in that short-as-fuck dress, you're gonna get hit on."

"I'm counting on it."

"That's my girl." Dare sticks out his fist. We fist bump. "Okay, ladies, ready to get this show on the road?"

"Ready." Rue waves her hand. She's holding on to her phone. Her screen lights up. A notification.

She looks at her phone.

"Shit."

"What?" I ask.

"Trace follows me on Insta. He liked this post." She holds up her phone in front of my face.

The picture is a wide shot of Dare with his fingers in my hair. His other hand is on my hip.

"It's a good picture," I say.

"That's not the problem. Trace shared the post. Guess who follows him?"

"I doubt he cares."

"Leigh, he beat the shit out of Shay for showing you his magic trick."

"Who beat who over a magic trick? Was it a good trick? Will Riley like it?"

We all look at Midnight.

He flips the hood of his hoodie over his head, looking like a thug. "What?" He nods at the door. "Come on. The quicker we get this done, the faster we can get to the fun stuff."

"Fun stuff?" I shouldn't have asked.

Midnight tilts his head back at the winding staircase. "Have you seen *Princess Diaries*, Leigh?"

"Heard of it. Not my kind of movie."

"No kidding?"

"None."

He rubs his hands together. There's a shit-eating grin on his face. Crap.

"Well, you see, there's this kickass slumber party, and the princess and her friends take turns going down the stairs riding atop a mattress."

"What's so fun about that?"

Red, Rue, and Dare shout, "We go down naked!"

The unnamed condition I agreed to when Rue said Midnight and Dare are more than willing to help.

My scars.

Crap. Crap. Crap.

26

*T*he party at Galley Rutherford's is unlike any party I've been at. And looks like something out of a movie. There are these spotlights set up on the lawn that point at the sky. Also a fog machine. Kids spill out of the house, onto the lawn, and onto the sidewalk.

"Wow, you weren't kidding about how big Galley's parties get, but what's the theme?"

I am in the middle seat of the middle row in Midnight's SUV. He and Dare are dropping us off, and then they'll join the party and jump in at the right moment.

"The Freaks Come Out At Night," Midnight answers.

Galley likes to hashtag his parties. Dare and

Midnight don't go to DU, but when your families are filthy rich, you tend to run in the same social circle.

"I wouldn't have guessed," Rue says. She is sitting to my left. Red is on my right. "Leigh, you sure Henry and his ex will be here?"

"Yep. I saw it on their feeds." I Insta-stalked them.

"Stop yapping already and get the hell out of the car," Dare says from his spot riding shotgun. "Go have fun but not too much. Easy on the alcohol too. Don't want you guys upchucking on the way down the stairs. That shit goes *everywhere*."

Rue and I shake our heads and follow Red out of the SUV. Teetering on my sky-high heels, I pull down the hem of my minidress. I am not about flaunting my body, but tonight is different. It's all about baiting a certain someone into cheating on his girlfriend.

Do I feel bad? Nope.

Henry's ex-girlfriend sure didn't put his feelings first when she hooked up with a guy who wasn't her boyfriend.

The three of us walk up to the house. The fog at our feet gives off the illusion of floating on clouds, while the fog lights lighting up the sky give off this weird glam vibe. It's like walking on clouds on our way to accepting an award, the take-down-cheaters trophy.

We walk up to the house.

Manning the front door are two muscular and tall guys wearing backward baseball caps. One has a sexy smirk, and the other is just as sexy, with his guns for arms and come-hither smile. The guys look us up and down. I have a few layers of makeup on, and so does Rue, but we still look youngish. Dare thought ahead and got us fake IDs and fake student IDs.

"Who you here with, girls?"

"Why ask just us? What about him?" I tip my head at Red.

"We didn't ask Red. We asked you."

"Who are you?" I cross my arms, and pulling back my shoulders, I straighten to my full height of five feet five inches.

The one with the sexy smirk scoffs. "I asked first."

A pissing match. Nice. I extend my hand and smile. "Name's Leigh. This is Rue."

The larger of the two guys leans in, intensely checking out Rue. "You look familiar."

"My sister goes here. Her name's Riley Lee."

The guys look at one another. "We know Riley. She's cool. It's nice to meet you two. Name's Xander.

This is Zeke. I'm Zeke and Galley's team captain. Rugby. Don't want no trouble, so you girls have fun. Grab me or Zeke if any guy gives you a hard time, got that? No guy has the right to harass a girl when she's only here for fun times."

"We will," I say. "Thank you."

They let us through the door. Zeke smiles and gives us a two-finger salute. I almost swoon at his feet. My oh my, that boy is panty-melting hot. Me and Rue walk inside the house arm in arm. Red is busy fist bumping and shoulder bumping Xander and Zeke.

"Have you ever been to a party of this magnitude?" I ask, embarrassed to have used a big word, but there is no other word to describe how impressed I am. I'm excited too.

"Never. This is true adulting."

Smiling, I lean into her. "Our first experience adulting together. This is awesome."

"Agreed."

We walk deeper into the house. To our right is the kitchen, and it is crowded in there.

"Want to get something to drink?" Rue asks. "Dare says they keep the kegs outside on these benches. It's easier to get them out there than through the crowd."

That makes sense. We shuffle to the kitchen. Bodies push into us and I hold on to Rue's arm. Red follows close behind us. Outside, we stand in line and wait our turn.

After we get our drinks and I get some liquid courage in me, we split up. I have my cell and fake IDs tucked into the front of my dress. Sipping my drink, I do an "inventory" of the partygoers. I have this fascination for people watching.

While I watch people mosh in the mosh pit and grind on one another next to the jumping and head-banging partygoers, my forehead tingles. I take a small sip of my beer and slide my eyes upward. A tall guy with a hoodie over his head stares at me from across the room.

Midnight.

He tips his chin. Is Dare behind me? Or is it Ashley's boyfriend? I pivot slowly on my heels, hoping I'm coming off casual rather than ogling. There are so many good-looking guys here.

I spot him right away. It's easy spotting Ashley's new boyfriend in the crowd. He tops the guys by a good four inches. Not only is he tall but I have to say he is the best-looking guy at this party. Dirty-blond hair. Bright-green eyes. He catches me staring, and giving me a flirty smile, he strokes his jaw and hooks his thumb in his pants pocket, looking suave and sexy.

I smile back over the rim of my red cup. He heads over. Ashley is MIA, but Henry isn't. I saw him out back. He doesn't realize I'm here yet. He will soon.

"Hey, there."

I point at my chest.

"Yeah, you." His smile widens. "What's your name?"

"Leigh."

"Nice to meet you, Leigh. Name's Jackson." He sticks out his hand. I set my hand in his. He holds on and doesn't let go.

"Are you a freshman? I haven't seen you on campus."

Huh, and here I thought he would only have eyes for his *girlfriend*.

"A transfer from California. I came to the party hoping to meet new people. It's hard to make friends when everyone has their own group already."

I make a sad face. His arm wraps around my waist, and he pulls me against his side.

"I can show you around campus and Dumas."

"Really?" I amp up the excitement in my voice. Then drop it down to a note of disappointment. "Wouldn't your girlfriend mind? I mean, a guy like you must have one. You are hot." I glance up at him and bat my eyelashes.

"I don't do girlfriends." He stares at my cleavage. "I'm into fuck buddies only."

Whoa. This guy tells it like it is. I widen my eyes and turn into him, resting the hand holding the red cup on his chest.

"Is that what you'd like us to be?"

"If you're up for it."

"I'm not the prettiest girl at this party."

"You are to me." He ducks his head and in my ear whispers, "Say yes."

"What if people find out? I don't like anyone in my business. And I'm new. I don't want guys thinking I'm easy just because I agree to be your willing hole."

God, saying those words make me feel so dirty.

He cups my waist. Fingers press into my skin through my dress. "It'll be our secret. I promise."

Bam. Hook, line, and sinker, I have him. Now on to the next act.

"*W*hen can we start?" I say breathless-like. "Unless you're playing with me. Guys can be worse than girls, teasing and promising things, then not following through."

"Is that so? You have experience with this?"

"On my knees kind of experience," I purr.

"Fuck, you are hot."

"And in need of liquid courage. I'm more limber when I'm wasted." I edge back.

He licks his lips, his eyes hanging on my mouth. Is he wondering what I can do with my mouth? Here is crossing my fingers he does. Also, Midnight or Dare better be getting all this on video. I am uncomfortable as heck flirting with a guy like I'm a hussy.

If I had my way, I would be talking to Seven in this way rather than this cheating jerk.

"I can help you with that. Let me refill this baby for you." He takes my cup. I follow him outside. He tells me to wait by the door. I see the reason. Henry is outside talking to this pretty gal with long brown hair. She is smiling at him, hanging on his every word.

As though he feels me staring a hole into the back of his head, Henry turns around. When he sees me, his eyes get huge. I give him a big smile and a small wave, tugging at the hem of my dress when it rises.

Jackson returns and hands me my cup. Out of the corner of my eye, Henry's jaw locks and his body pulls taut. I take the cup from Jackson, murmur a breathless, "Thank you, big guy," and chug my drink.

"Ready?"

I nod. He leads me out of the kitchen, and bumping into other partiers who barely glance our way, he guides me up the stairs. Whatever he refilled my cup with is stronger. I'm tipsy and woozy, my body buzzing.

"Did you put something in my drink?"

"You wanted liquid courage. I added tequila."

Shit, no wonder I am swimming in a daze of drunkenness. I'm a lightweight. It's the reason I sipped my drink and to chug beer and however much tequila Jackson mixed into my drink . . .

I stumble on the carpet. He picks me up. The room is *spinning*. Oh, God, this is such a bad idea. I rub my brow. Close my eyes. Every step he takes ups my dizziness factor by twofold. Where is Henry? Where are Midnight and Dare? Rue I saw talking to a bunch of guys with Red at her side.

Jackson stops walking. I open my eyes, and my vision adjusts to the darkness. He sets me on my feet and takes my cup from me, setting it on top of a bookcase. The whooping and hollering from downstairs fades, then mutes altogether when Jackson shuts the bedroom door.

"We shouldn't be up here. It's some other guy's room."

"He won't care, baby." He pushes me onto the bed.

I try sitting up. The room spins, and I fall back onto the bed. He comes over to the side of the bed and looks at me, starting from my heels to my bare legs to the rise and fall of my chest. He leans in and skims his fingers over the swells of my breasts.

"Small. Sexy."

He trails his fingers down the center of my body. When he gets to the hem of my dress, he uses both hands and hitches up my dress until the hem pools around my waist. He drinks in my white thong with his eyes.

Where is Henry? Did I have this all wrong, that Henry will come to my rescue knowing what a douchebag Jackson is?

The door crashes open, and slinging my arm across my eyes, I smiled shakily. Thank the stars.

There's a scuffle, followed by the sound of a body hitting a piece of furniture, hard. Holy cow, Henry is strong. And pissed off. I lift my arm. It's not Henry taking on douchebag Jackson. Jackson staggers out of the room. Dark-as-coal eyes blaze angry and hot at me, Seven's gaze eating me up.

He marches to the bed, and before I can get a word in, he picks me up and slings me over his shoulder.

"Seven?"

"Not a word, Leigh. I am so pissed at you right now."

"No, shit, Sherlock."

"Put a sock on it, Defiance."

"You're telling me to shut up?"

"Yeah, I did. Not a word, Leigh, or else I hike up this damn dress of yours and show everyone your ass."

That shuts me up fast. On our way out the door, I bypass Henry. Dare, Midnight, Rue, and Red look on with curiosity and amusement. Henry is pissed.

"Where were you guys?" My words slur. I glare. Dare opens his mouth.

A heavy hand smacks my ass. I suck in a breath. Dare shuts his mouth. I don't miss the gleam in his eyes. Boys. I am done with them.

Sighing, I hang my head. Not difficult to do slung over Seven's shoulder like prey after a successful hunt. I shouldn't be mad at Seven or my new friends. Compared to Jackson, they are golden.

"What are you doing here?"

He ignores my question, walking for what seems like forever before he stops in front of his truck parked blocks from the party.

He sets me on my feet. "You need to throw up at all?"

I'm in awe he's not out of breath carrying me the distance. This boy has stamina and strength. Believe me, I am not light. I shake my head.

"If you do, I have barf bags left over from when we came home from the hospital." He opens the passenger-side door. "Get in."

I tip my chin. He grasps my chin and tilts my face up.

"I'm done with your defiance, beautiful. You are mine. Now *please* get your ass inside before I put you over my knee and spank obedience into you."

For him saving me from being a number on Jackson's list of random screws, I climb inside Seven's truck. He gets in, starts the engine, and gets on the road.

"Explain what the hell you're doing at a party getting ready for some guy to crawl up on you?"

"I don't owe you one. Why are you in Dumas, anyway?"

"Take a guess, Leigh. It has something to do with you letting that fucker Dare touch you."

Shit, the IG post of Rue's.

"We were testing a theory, that's all."

"He had his hands all over you. All over what's mine."

"I'm not yours."

"Keep telling yourself that, Defiance."

We sit in tense silence. I ball my hands in my lap. He's right. I would be lying if I said I didn't want to be Seven Shanahan's girlfriend.

"Where are we going?" He took a turn onto a side road lined with these cute houses that look like cottages out of a fairy tale.

"My place."

"Your parents have a house here?"

"I bought a place with the birthday money they gave me."

"You are one hundred percent certain you'll be going to DU."

"I plan on playing ball for them."

I chew on my bottom lip. He could be DU's next quarterback. King of the game. A new kingdom to rule over. His pick of girls. Why would he pick a girl with scars on her body? Who isn't a part of the popular crowd? I am outcast material. A rebel. I would never fall in line with his crowd of jocks and cheerleaders.

"That's great, Seven. You have your future all planned out." Swell. In that future picture is a beautiful cheerleader.

I should be glad he has his head on straight enough to know what he wants in his future. Then why does my heart break knowing I will never be a part of it?

*T*o say I am pissed is an understatement. I shove open the driver-side door, stomp over to Leigh, who did not listen when I told her to stay in the goddamn truck, and picking her up, I haul her over my shoulder.

"Seven, put me down."

I stop. "Why, you going to barf?"

"I'm too heavy."

Hearing how unhappy she is I'm here spoiling her fun, I set her back on her feet. "Don't think you can bolt," I tell her, bringing us back to that night I saved her from a drowning and carried her to her place. "I'll catch you every time."

"I hope so," I hear her mutter under her breath.

"Come on, let's get that mask off your face." I

extend my hand to her. She doesn't take it. Leigh crosses her arms. They're under her tits, pushing up on them, giving me an eyeful.

"You don't like my makeup?"

"I like you natural." I look her up and down. "*Bare.*"

"You made the drive to tell me that?"

"I made the drive to claim what's mine. You are mine, Leigh. Now come on, let's get out of the cold."

Thank fuck she puts her hand in mine. It's awkward as hell, and I look like a moron with my hand stuck out between us. We take the porch steps hand in hand. I let us inside my place.

"Bathroom is straight ahead, door to your right."

Leigh lets go of my hand, finds the bathroom, and to the delight of my dick, she comes out minutes later, her face bare of makeup. I skim my finger down the side of her face.

Soft. Smooth. *Mine.*

I lean in, and tucking strands of her hair behind her cute ear, I press my mouth on the curve of her ear and ask for an explanation for why she was at that damn party.

I'm surprised when she gives it. Surprised when my heart kicks up extra beats. This girl and how big her heart is for a dude who nearly killed her.

"Leigh, your intention is good, but you have to let people grow and learn from their mistakes. Henry knew Ashley wasn't with him for the right reason, and he stuck with her anyway."

"What do you mean?"

Sighing, I take her hand. "Do you mind if we finish this convo in bed? It's been a long day, and I'm ready to keel over."

Honest-to-God truth, I am not trying to get in Leigh's pants.

Between seeing that IG post of Leigh and Dare, overhearing my dad begging my mom to come home, and blaming yesterday's loss on losing my lucky coin, I am pushing my limit of being able to stand upright.

Not to mention I paid attention to the speed limit on the drive from Cambridge to Dumas when I'd rather floor the gas pedal. No way in hell will I risk crashing and burning and miss my chance to tell Leigh how pissed off I am that she let another dude touch her fine-ass body.

She nods, and I lead her to the bedroom. Inside, we lay fully clothed on top of the covers. I clasp her hand in mine.

"How are your knuckles?"

"Nothing for you to worry over." The swelling

went down after I iced it.

"Look, Leigh—" I turn on my side, needing to see her. "Ashley's grades weren't top notch, and to get into DU, a person needs to have top-notch grades, be a superstar jock, or have a huge financial need. Ashley doesn't fit any of those criteria."

"How'd she get in?"

"Henry helped her get the grades. Did her assignments."

"She used him."

"Yes."

"She misled him, using his feelings for her."

"He wasn't innocent in all this, Leigh. He understood what she was, a user, a manipulator."

"But he stuck around hoping to change her, and she didn't change. Instead, she went for the next best thing and broke his heart. Is that why you keep saying I'm yours? You want to change me, get me to fall in line, to bow to the king of the game? Show me you care when you don't? Mislead me?"

Fuck, she's onto me, and I'm a bastard. I open my mouth to tell her, but what she does next has me shutting the fuck up.

"I couldn't give a care anymore for your reasons, Seven. You're right. I want to just be and enjoy what

I have in the here and now. I am yours, Seven Shanahan. I. Am. All. Yours."

Her words shred my heart.

She is mine.

I'll never be hers.

The almighty ruler of Cambridge High bows down to no one, not even a five-foot-five girl with attitude and a big heart.

*A*fter I told Seven I am his, we stripped to our underwear and fell asleep in each others' arms, too tired and emotionally drained to do much about our half-naked state and our hormones.

The next day, Henry stopped by Seven's quaint place. I don't know how he knew where Seven took me, but he did. We talked, and I apologized for meddling in his life. He said next time I plan on meddling, give him a heads up. He freaked out big time seeing Jackson leading me up the stairs. Before he could storm inside the bedroom, Seven beat him to it.

The video Midnight took of Jackson and me circulated online. Interestingly, Ashley stuck with

Jackson. We later found out Ashley was hooking up with a different guy, and that was her reason for not being at the party. Wow, just wow. Those two are meant to be together. I hope they use protection. Talk about STD city.

At school on Monday, Hannah pulls me into a hug, having heard from Henry what I did for him.

Her welcoming me like that sent a message to the rest of the students. Leigh is my friend. Mess with her and you mess with me and my kickass cheerleaders. I like being wanted, but that doesn't mean I am for Team Hannah. I have my own set of friends.

During math class, one of the office staff walks in holding a vase of red roses. She walks to my row of desks. I wait for her to walk past. She stops at my desk and sets the vase down.

Everyone looks at me. The back of my head tingles. Not giving a care that the entire class is watching, including the teacher, I open the envelope and slide out the card.

"I'm sorry, Leigh. S." I slip the card back inside, happiness blooming warm across my chest.

Seven apologizing for what he did to Shay, for being a jerk in front of my new friends. I fight back the urge to turn in my seat and tell him thank you.

It's dumb, but I want him to be the first to tell the world that I am his and he is my guy. Even signing the card with the first letter of his name isn't cutting it. Call me old-fashioned, but I am after a public declaration.

When the last bell rings, I hurry to my locker. I see Seven walking away from my locker, his backpack hitched high on his shoulder. Walking next to him is Ginger.

She must have said something funny. Seven laughs. His arm slides across her small shoulders, and he pulls her to him. Am I wrong, and the roses aren't from him?

My chest aching, I open my locker, suddenly not excited to go to Seven's practice. Slipped inside my locker is a piece of paper. I unfold the paper and read Seven's words with tears stinging the corners of my eyes.

Ginger is tutoring me now. Thanks for the help. See you around. Seven.

See you around? Cold settles over my body. I grab my backpack out of my locker, shove my books inside, and trash the vase and the roses in the nearest trash can.

Torn up inside, I hurry from the school and board the bus, grabbing the last seat at the back of the bus. Pitying glances all around from the other kids. My face must've said it all. Or they only need to look out the bus windows. Seven has his arm across Ginger's shoulders, and she's wearing his letterman jacket.

I duck my head and stare at my shaking hands clasped in my lap. Well, damn, I didn't see that one coming. And it only gets worse from there.

The rest of the week plays out like that. Seven doesn't acknowledge I exist. As soon as I said the words, "I am all yours," I sealed my fate.

There isn't much more of me he wants. There are prettier, smarter girls out there. Girls who follow the rules. A girl who won't rock the boat. Someone who fits perfectly in his crowd.

The only good that's come out of Seven's rejection is my growing friendship with Hannah. She comes over and hangs out at my place. We do cool things like make jewelry and put on these fake tattoos we ordered online. We also bake like crazy.

The bad? I have to know more about Ginger. At first, Hannah didn't want to tell, but after I told her I'll go with when she gets her first *real* tattoo, she caved.

"Ginger's parents own the town center. They graduated from DU."

"So she'll be going there, too?"

"4.0 GPA, and she's a track star."

Double whammy for me. Ginger is the perfect girl for Seven.

"Thanks for being my friend, Hannah. I appreciate you coming over and baking with me."

"Carbs solve all the problems of the world, don't they?"

"For sure." I bite into a gooey cookie. "How are things with Cam?"

"Good. He's taking me to homecoming."

"That's cool."

"And we FaceTimed Henry and gave him the news."

"How'd he handle it?"

"Well. He's seeing someone new. A girl he met at a party. He says she's really nice and down to earth."

"I'm happy for him."

"Me too. Ready to bake brownies?"

Nodding, I shove another cookie in my mouth. Nothing like stress eating. Too bad the carbs don't take away the ache in my chest.

I miss Seven.

*T*he next week is the same sad story. Except it's different for one big reason— homecoming. It's all everyone is talking about, though the homecoming game and the dance isn't until the next Friday.

I don't have money for a dress. I don't have the enthusiasm to go. I'll be a horrible date. Shay disagrees.

"Think about it, Shay, you can go with the girl of your dreams rather than because you did it to piss Seven off. He doesn't care. Doesn't hate me anymore. I cease to exist in his eyes."

I lean against the window of his sportscar. He is parked alongside the fence, and we're facing the turn in the road that forks right to Seven's parents' place.

"Fuck's sake, Leigh, stop being so dramatic."

"It's true," I whine.

"Then get him to hate you again."

"I don't want his hate."

"You fell for him, didn't you? Don't know what you see in the guy. He's a jerk."

"He's not."

I tell him of how Seven took me to the hospital and stayed with me. How he cared for me, feeding me, and making sure I didn't keel over. Also, harped on me to take the antibiotics. I also tell him what Seven does for the poorer kids.

"Then what's the problem? Why are you moping?"

"He's interested in a different girl. It's the reason he doesn't hate me anymore. He's too busy paying attention to her now."

I tell Shay of how Seven ditched me for Ginger.

"I'm sorry, Leigh."

"I'll get over it." I won't. Not for awhile. "So, you'll ask Blair to the dance?"

"I already did, a week before Brody's party. She turned me down, said she's not into those things."

"It's senior year. Last homecoming dance. Ask her again."

"Drop it, Leigh."

I shift in my seat. His fingers are crammed in his hair.

"Or ask what she'd rather do. If she's not into a dance, what about a picnic under the moonlight? Or stargazing? Ask her, Shay. Do something she'd like to do."

His hand falls from his hair. He skims his fingers over the steering column, looking thoughtful. "You're onto something. I'll ask. What about you?"

"I'll go to the game but not the dance."

"Sorry things got out of hand at Brody's party."

"Hey, never be sorry for showing me a magic trick. I'll love them all."

He laughs. "Promise?"

"Promise."

"You're the sweetest girl, Leigh. If Seven doesn't see what's right in front of him and come around, it's his loss."

Tired of fighting the fight inside me alone, I lean into him and rest my head on his shoulder. "Thank you for being my friend. For giving me a ride back from the shop."

Surprise, surprise, Shay works at the auto store too.

"Anytime. That's what friends are for, isn't it? To be there for one another?"

Then where is Seven in all this?

Mid-week, I get news I'm not ready for. What Maddox tells me sets my world off-kilter. Makes me believe less in love. Makes me question my beliefs of what my parents had. Has me questioning whether what my mom told Alistair is the truth, that Thomas is my biological father.

"Leigh." Maddox shoves his fingers in his hair. We're on video chat, and in the window behind him is a view of the Golden Gate Bridge.

"Leigh, I've got shitty news. Leigh, you're going to hate me. Leigh . . ."

God, when he keeps saying my name like that, with pity, I know the news is really, really bad, like vomit-inducing bad.

"Leigh, your mom filed for divorce. She and Tony planned on getting married."

"That's a lie."

"Leigh, my guy talked to Tony's brother. He said your mom and Tony were in love. They met when Tony answered a call of a break-in at the shop your mother worked at sewing those pretty dresses of hers."

"He's lying. My mother loved my father. She said he was her soul mate."

"Believe what you want, kiddo, but your denial doesn't make the divorce papers go away."

I swallow down the bile in my throat. It wasn't my obedience that got my mom and Alistair killed. It was my *defiance*, going back on my promise to my mom that I would never tell my dad about Tony.

If I hadn't told, Alistair wouldn't have driven us to the police station, confronted Tony, and got him and Mom killed when he pulled out his gun and Mom shielded him, getting shot too when the officers returned fire.

Oh, God, my defiance cost my parents their lives. "What else?"

"Tony and that kid Seven, his dad, Six . . . Six is Tony's half-brother, Leigh. Six is the result of an affair, a bastard child, but no less an heir to the McCabe empire."

Seven is related to the man who destroyed my family?

"I looked into the woman who was in the hotel room with Six. They were engaged. Word is she's looking to reconnect."

"In his hotel room? He's married."

"She's not, and old flames die hard. I'm sorry."

Hearing all this, finally processing that falling in love hurts and true love is never a guarantee, what my mom taught me when I was a little girl, the floodgates open. I burst out crying. Poor Maddox tugs at his collar.

"Leigh, please don't cry."

I cry harder. I want Seven. Long to tell him how wrong I was about my parents. That they were never in love the way I thought they were, happily and unconditionally.

My mother cheated on my father. Was divorcing him. She lied to me. Lied to all of us. Lied and misled my kindhearted father. The father who spent time in prison because he knew I needed my EpiPen, a medication we couldn't afford. He stole for me. He died for love. What did my soft-spoken mother do? She betrayed me. Got her and my dad killed for love and betrayal. Damn her.

"Leigh, kiddo, please, you're breaking my heart seeing you cry like this."

"I hate this. Hate him."

"Who?"

"Seven. I hate him for making me feel things. For believing in something that doesn't exist for me."

"Leigh, your feelings are important, but you're

only eighteen, kiddo. What does someone your age know about love?"

"Were you ever in love, M?"

"Yes, kiddo, I was."

"What happened?"

"She broke my heart."

"How old were you?"

"Eighteen." He scrubs his hand over his face. "You made your point. Hang tight, kiddo, I'm coming for my sex tapes."

*M*addox convinced me to play hooky from school tomorrow and Friday. I didn't want to miss my shift at Queenie's on Friday, but after hearing how scratchy and shaky my voice is, Miles tells me to take Friday off, that it's only four hours.

After getting off the phone with Miles, I trudge over to Seven's place. Maddox will be here in half an hour. In front of his door, I knock. It takes a few minutes before he opens the door. I can see why. Behind him is Ginger. They must have been studying. Probably in his bedroom.

"Seven, can I speak with you?" I keep my head down, not wanting him to see my puffy face. I am such an ugly crier.

"Yeah, sure. I'll be right back, Ginger."

Wow, he was never that nice with me. If it were me in Ginger's place, he would say something like, "Don't you bolt, Leigh. I'll catch you every time."

I sigh. I miss him.

"What's up?"

He sticks his hands in his pockets. He is wearing dark blue jeans. Bare feet. We're out on his front porch. The porch is a dark wood. There's a white porch swing. Pots of flowers in the corners. So romantic. I could sit on the swing and be happy staring off at the countryside day or night. Night would be awesome. The crickets and frogs would make their cute mating calls.

"Leigh?"

"I . . . Um, Maddox called me."

"And?"

"He didn't find anything. I'm sorry." It's easy to lie. I'm saving Seven from the devastation I went through when Maddox told me something that destroyed my belief in what my parents had. I can't destroy whatever chance Seven thinks his parents have of reconciling.

"You should talk to your dad, Seven. Tell him how you're feeling. Or don't and let them work through their problems."

"You don't think my dad was set up like your mom was?"

"Seven—" Tears burn the back of my eyes.

I should go; I don't want Seven to see how hard I've fallen for him or how much he hurt me when I told him I'm his only to have him throw my loyalty in my face when he got what he wanted. But I have to say my piece.

"Seven, I'm not in the right place to give you advice," I admit. "What your parents are going through, it could be as simple and complex as one person still in love with the other and the other wants out."

Without looking at him, I reach inside my pocket and pull out what I never had a right to let someone else take from him.

"Here's your lucky coin." I stretch out my hand. "You'll need it Friday."

"How—"

"Red is my friend. He understands how important this coin is to you. He's doing it for me and not you."

He takes the coin from me.

I turn and, over my shoulder, say words that end whatever it was we had.

"See you around, Seven."

*T*he sun is bright, and the sand is soft beneath my bare feet.

Maddox brought me to St. Thomas, one of the Virgin Islands, on his private jet. We arrived early Thursday morning, was picked up at the airport and taken to his house that sits a few feet from the beach.

I drape my towel over the back of the lounge chair, sit, and stretching out my legs, I tug the wide-brim straw hat down over my eyes. A large figure looms over me.

"Get in the water, Leigh."

"It's too early."

"It's noon."

"I'm tired."

"You're in need of cheering up." Maddox knocks

the hat off my head, ditches the sunglasses that take up half my face, and picking me up under my arms, he slings me over his shoulder.

"Put me down."

"No. You have a dark cloud of sadness over your pretty head, and I intend on dunking the doom and gloom off you."

"I don't need cheering up. I like the doom and gloom. Put me down." I pound on his back.

He laughs.

"Jesus, M, you can be such a jerk."

"Am I, Leigh? Who jetted you off to paradise?" He marches farther out into the water with ease. The ocean should be resisting his body. His body is built of solid muscles.

"Answer the questions, Leigh."

"No, you're not a jerk. You're my friend."

"You're damn right I'm your friend. Never forget that."

He dumps me in the water. I land with a loud *plunk*. Closing my eyes, I take in the warm water on my face and the tendrils of my hair floating around me. The sun high in the sky is a change from the cold and the rain back in Cambridge.

Smiling at how good the heat feels, I come up for air and run my palm over my face. Thick fingers tuck my hair behind my ears. I open my eyes. Blink. Look up into the most gorgeous blue-green eyes. He smiles at me. I smile back, and pushing off the sand, I throw my arms around Maddox's neck.

"You're a good friend. Thank you, M, for bringing me here."

His arms wrap around my waist, and he tugs me close. "If you want to cry, I won't judge, Leigh."

"I miss him."

"It gets better. The feelings will fade."

"I'll see him at school for the next eight months. He lives next door. I'll see him driving by in his truck. The truck he let me stay in during his practices to keep me from freezing my ass off."

"I understand, kiddo. You don't want to forget. You want to remember how he made you feel wanted and special."

"Is that bad?" I bury my face in the curve of his neck.

"It's never bad to be wanted. Or to feel like you're important to someone, a part of their life."

"It hurts. Him. My parents. In my eyes, they were the perfect couple. The princess and her bad boy, the one who would do anything to make her life easier. They were each other's best friends too."

"Just because you're wrong about them doesn't

mean you have to be wrong about love. Kiddo, you have the rest of your life to fall in and out of love."

I blow out a breath. "Why do you keep calling me kiddo? We're only six years apart."

He walks us farther out. His hands on my waist, he hoists me up. I wrap my legs around his waist.

"You know why? You are a lot like my little sis. Tough on the outside. Soft on the inside. Doesn't break for no one, but when she does and she gets hurt, that outer shell is difficult for anyone to get past the next go around. I don't want that for you, Leigh. I don't want this guy Seven to mess it up for other guys. You get where I'm coming from?"

"You don't want me to fortify my shell with layers and layers of steel. You don't want me to be cynical and bitter."

"Yes."

I smile. "Why couldn't you have just said, stay strong, Leigh? Keep your chin up, Leigh? Keep being a tough cookie, Leigh?"

"That would be too easy. Speaking of cookie, you hungry?"

"Is there a place we can get pho?"

"If not, I'll have it flown in."

I hug him tighter. "If I could have anyone as my big brother, it'd be you, M."

"Aw, shucks, kiddo, that means the world to me. But promise me something?"

"Sure."

"If you're gonna steal one of my rides, go with the least expensive one, okay?"

Staring into bright blue-green eyes, I laugh. "I promise."

"THANKS again for whisking me off to paradise, M." We're sitting inside his private jet, headed back to Washington state. By the time we arrive, it will be close to midnight.

"Feel better?"

"Yes." I do. I really do.

The sunshine, the shops, the nightlife, all of it lifted my spirits and gave my mind a rest from facing Seven, the upcoming "Spirit Week," and the homecoming dance I won't be going to but he will with his new girl, Ginger.

On the table between us, Maddox's cellphone rings. He takes the call. His mood goes from happy to high-in-the-stratosphere pissed off.

"What the fuck? You're telling me someone bypassed my security system and blew up my garage?" He shoves his fingers through his hair. "You think it has something to do with what's on TMZ? Fuck sakes, I don't keep up with that shit. Send me the link."

He ends the call. His phone beeps. Maddox opens the link and drops a string of f-bombs.

"What is it?"

He slides his phone over to me. I pick it up and look at the screen. There is a short article in TMZ, a tabloid news site, with the headlines, "The Billionaire and His Newest Girlfriend Frolicking on the Beach."

There are pictures upon pictures of me and Maddox in the ocean with our arms around one another. With my face buried in his hair. Him planting a kiss on the top of my head, my forehead, my nose. His arms under my ass as he walked us out of the water that second day at the beach.

"Frolicking. That's a dumb word." I set his phone on the table. "We lived it up, that's what we did."

He doesn't answer. He stares straight ahead with his hands tented over his mouth. I place my hand on his knee. "Are you ashamed that they made me out to be your girl? You can have your PR person get ahold of them and deny it. I won't be put out, M."

"I don't give a shit that TMZ claims you're my

girl. What I give a fuck about is someone destroyed my cars. Should I make your guy pay? Or should we celebrate his show of affection for you, kiddo?"

"Seven blowing up your precious collection doesn't mean jack shit." I cross my arms.

Maddox pulls me into his lap, grabs my chin, and forces me to look at him. "His father's family is dangerous. They have the means to fuck me up. Shit, Leigh, they destroyed property, going unnoticed. That is power. They don't wield it without cause. Love is enough cause for them to do this for him. Accept his declaration."

"Destruction is never the answer. Destruction isn't love." My throat tightens. My voice is scratchy. Crap, I am going to bawl.

"Promise me you'll listen to what he has to say? Give him another chance if he asks for it. Will you do that?"

"For you losing more cars because of me, I will."

33

*T*he first thing my father did after hearing of what I'd asked of my cousins is to sit me down and demand I talk to him.

"What the fuck is going on, Seven?"

I pace, refusing to open up to the man who ruined a good thing. Why did he give up on Mom so easily after she put up with his drinking for years as he wrestled with the darker side of his job? Why did he put himself in the position of getting caught with another woman? Shit, why put himself in that position in the first place?

But the more he looked at me with love in his eyes as he followed my movements, the words spilled from me like a dam broken by too much pressure placed on it.

I start with my anger over him messing things up with Mom.

"Did you fall out of love with her?"

"None of that."

"Did you cheat on her?"

"Never."

"Then what the fuck is the problem?"

"Fuck sakes, Seven, watch the fucking language."

I smirk. Yeah, sure, I'll watch it when he curbs his love for the f-bomb too.

"Your mom's changed, Son. She's been withdrawn. Hasn't opened up to me the way she used to. I went to see Marianne, hoping she could shed some light on why. Marianne, she and I, we were engaged. She was your mom's best friend."

"Wait, what? You were caught half-naked in a hotel room with a woman you were planning on marrying?"

What the fuck?

"What Marianne and I had was an arranged marriage, the joining of two powerful families. But when I met your mom, all bets were off. She was all I thought about. The thing is, your mother is the purest of heart, too kind for this damn world. She's a force for good, and I've done nothing but wrong her, keeping truths from her."

He sets his elbows on his knees and drops his head in his palms.

It takes a lot for my dad to open up to me like this. What he told me, about my mom withdrawing from him, goes beyond the normal father-and-son talk. I give him my truth.

"Dad, you haven't wronged her. There's nothing wrong with loving someone the way you and Mom love one another. What is wrong is you working so much we barely see you. What is wrong is you not involving Mom in your line of work anymore."

They fought about that part, very loudly. Mom used to help with the "family" business of this foreign trade thing of Dad's until Dad told my mom to stay out of it. That his line of work is getting too dangerous for her.

"Mom has a degree in computer science. Large companies come to her to hack their systems for flaws. Use her skills. Mom wants to be useful, to make a difference, to help."

I take a seat next to him.

"Does Mom know the marriage was arranged?"

"No."

"You should tell her the reason Marianne was in your room."

"She set me up."

287

"What?" I ask, the agony in Dad's voice threatening to have me send my cousins after this Marianne chick.

"She's still in love with me. Can't forgive your mom for agreeing to marry me. Hates me for ending our engagement. She had a photographer take the picture. I didn't know she was in the room until it was too late. We were supposed to meet in the hotel's lounge."

"Tell Mom this."

"I'd have to tell her the rest. How I set up the assault. Me rescuing her. Me seducing her. Destruction and manipulation are all I've known growing up under the heavy hand of my dad, your grandfather Sean McCabe. Your grandmother gave me her name. I pass on the Shanahan name to you, but we will always be a McCabe, my father's name. The name and power you used to destroy Maddox Stassi's collection of exotic cars."

I hear every part of his speech but focus on the one thing that'll lighten the mood.

"Fuck sakes, Dad, I don't need to hear how you got in Mom's pants. Confess. Let her decide the next steps."

"How'd you get so wise?" He ruffles my hair. I smack his hand away, the heaviness in my chest lifting. My parents have another chance to get back what they lost. I'm crossing my fingers my mom believes my dad is worth a second chance.

"I'm far from wise, Dad. I hurt a girl I like. Am misleading a girl for the sake of making the other girl hate me more."

"How about we both take your advice, then regroup here tonight unless I get lucky and your mom invites me to stay over."

I stick my finger in my mouth and make a gagging noise. Dad laughs. Smiling, I stick out my fist for a fist bump. "Deal. Good luck, Dad."

"You too, Son. If everything goes well, invite her over. I'd like to meet the girl who got my son's panties in a bunch enough to destroy another man's expensive toys."

"Ha-ha, old man. Will do."

There's a knock on my door. Huh. That's odd. Well, it's not. Ever since that TMZ article blew up on the internet, there's been a line of people at my door.

First, Thomas. He insisted he give me the birds and the bees talk. Awkward. Next was Eleanor and Hannah wanting the scoop on my hot billionaire boyfriend. After that, Red, Rue, and Shay stopped by. They brought Winslow. He had demanded he meet the newest addition to their "crew." Nice. I liked him instantly, pairing him in my mind with Sorrow.

With his light-blond hair and her raven locks, they would be day and night. The dark knight climbing the tower to rescue his princess. I'll have to show Sorrow a picture of him when I go over later tonight. It's her birthday, and I have a gift, plus I'm baking a cake.

I hurry to the door and yank it open, thinking it's Miles. His father is closing the diner tonight, and Miles was stopping by with shakes. Cake and shakes for Sorrow's birthday. Yum.

Except it's not Miles. It's Seven.

"Seven, what are you doing here?"

When Maddox dropped me off at my place and insisted he walk me to my door, I knew there was an ulterior motive. He wanted to try, for the fifth time, to convince me to go speak with Seven. Uh-uh. It wasn't me who ended the friendship. Seven did. If he has something to say, he can do it to my face rather than blow up Maddox's cars.

"I brought you these."

He tips his head at the ground. I step forward and peek around the door. The outside lights are on, and they highlight the rose bushes in these cardboard planters as though to say, "Ta-da, he comes bearing gifts."

"They're ready to plant. Tell me where and I'll dig the holes."

I straighten and cross my arms. "It's six and I have somewhere to be." Nonchalant. Not affected at all by his gift.

"Where?"

But goodness, those puppy eyes. Jesus.

"A friend's." Oh, thank God my voice is steady.

"A guy's?"

I tip my chin. Am ready to tap my feet on the floor. "It's none of your business. Again, why are you here?"

"Can I come inside?" He shoves his hands inside his pockets and pulls his shoulders inward, looking broken and defeated.

"Seven, it's not a good idea."

"Leigh, please. Give me five minutes of your time. That's all I'm asking for."

"Five minutes." I step aside and wave him through. He plops down on the couch and stretches out his long legs. I offer him soda or water.

"Water's good. Thanks, Leigh."

I bring him a glass of water and pop open the tab of my can of soda. I sit on the far corner, opposite him.

"Smells good in here. Whatcha baking?"

Small talk is good.

"Angel food cake. It's my friend's eighteenth birthday."

"Cool. That's nice of you." He wipes his palms on his pants. Up. Down. Up. Down.

Is Seven nervous?

"You owe Maddox an apology, Seven."

"I don't owe him jack shit. He had his hands on my girl. My girl, Leigh."

Oh, no, he did not. I stand.

"Yours? You dare say I'm yours when you hurt me? Broke my heart when you ditched me and found someone else to take my spot?"

I ball my hands at my sides. He stands and reaches for me. I back up. He advances. The anger and determination on his face . . . I skirt around the table. He stalks after me. I make a mad dash for my bedroom. He chases me, and before I can shut the door on him, he barges his way inside my room.

Grabbing me by the shoulders, he pushes me onto the bed. He climbs on the bed and traps me in place with his thighs straddling my waist.

"Seven." I growl out a warning. "You have no right. No right to be here. To insert yourself in my life again. I have friends. Guys who are interested in me. All I have to do is give them the word and they are mine."

"Do it, Leigh. I'll fuck them up."

"*Seven.*"

He stretches out his legs, and sliding his body

over mine, he shifts us until I'm looking down into his dark eyes.

"Leigh, I'm sorry. I fucked up. Got scared of what I feel for you."

He's sincere. Honest. Broken. But I'm not ready to forgive him. I was sincere and honest too, and he left me broken when he sent me the roses only to slip a note in my locker telling me he's done with me.

"I hate you."

"You have every right. Let me tell my side, Leigh. Please."

Again, more begging.

"Tell."

As though he thinks I'll bolt, he swaps our position back to him on top of me. He keeps his weight off me with his arms alongside my head. Pieces of hair brush his forehead. I have this crazy urge to swipe aside the strands. I lock my arms against my sides. There will be no touching the jerk. He hurt me, and I'm not done hurting or hating on him.

"Leigh, it was my idea to get you to tutor me. My grades were in the shitter, like you said. Coach told me he was benching me for the next game. I went to the principal. He suggested a tutor. I gave him your name in the hopes I could mess with you more. Get your ass in the cold and the rain. Break you of your defiance. Get you to fall for me during our time together. Then when I knew you'd fallen for me, I'd drop you and break your heart."

He doesn't say any more. Just looks off to the side. He's ashamed and remorseful for toying with my feelings and messing with my mind. I should hate him more, but the thing is, what he's telling me isn't that terrible after hearing of what my mom did to Alistair.

I nudge him back to looking at me again with my knuckle on his chin. "Go on. What else?"

"I fell hard for you, Leigh. You became all I thought about. Filled my world. My life. Saw me for me. Became my sounding board without me feeling like less of a dude for showing you my softer side."

"I don't understand, Seven. If you fell hard for me, why ditch me?" Then I give him my truth. "I looked forward to spending time with you. Loved watching you do your thing on the field. Loved that you would rather come in through my window because at first, it started as something to get back at me for. Later, it became a part of us."

"Kind of like our pinky swears?" Small smile

from him, and my breath hitches in my chest. I miss Seven's smiles.

"Yes." My arms leave my sides. Wrap around his shoulders. Move down his back and settle on his waist. He is solid. Sexy. Could be mine again. "Why ditch me, Seven?"

He blows out a breath.

"It's stupid, but being around you distracted me. I couldn't study worth a damn. Couldn't play worth a damn either, losing my team games. I thought hanging with Ginger would make me forget you. That not hanging with you would help me play ball at top notch. But keeping away from you has done none of that. It wasn't you, Leigh. It was me."

He closes his eyes. Seems to be fighting this inner war with himself. I pull him down to me and rub my nose on his. Implore him to tell me what he means by it wasn't me but him. That I would never judge him no matter his answer. I care so much for him.

"You do?"

"Since the night you plucked me out of that pool."

"Aw, Leigh. God, seeing you in the water like that, I freaked out."

"You were so calm."

"Inside, I was shaking. Furious too."

"Thanks for telling me, Seven." I kiss him. He

kisses me back, putting everything into that kiss. His apology, remorse, fear, anger, happiness.

"Explain what you mean, Seven," I ask after we end our kiss with these endless pecks. "What did you mean, it's not me, that it was you?"

"I shouldn't have let what's going on with my parents distract me from playing ball at my top-notch best. Or make it an excuse to party and not do my schoolwork. Or believe that not having my lucky coin cost me games. It's on me for playing like shit."

He's accepting responsibility for his actions. Is acknowledging that he's made mistakes. I'm so proud of him, I want to throw my arms around him and keep kissing him. Except I let him talk. Seven needs to get everything off his chest.

"Or that you out of my life is the answer. It's not. Being with you is the only answer, Leigh. You listen. You help. You're kind. You're good. You're you, and damn if I don't like you for you."

He captures my mouth with his. I open to him, groaning beneath the onslaught of his mouth and his tongue. We kiss like this for what seems like forever, with a desperation of missing out on time with one another, of missing out on other chances to kiss and touch to our hearts' content. We break off the kiss with smiles on our faces.

"I'm sorry, Leigh, for everything. If you never forgive me, I'll understand."

"Thanks, Seven. I'm not ready."

"Will you ever be?"

"After more kisses. More nights of you climbing in through my window. More nights stargazing or listening to the rain on the skylight, snuggled up to you."

"Aw, babe. I care so much for you."

"I care too." I skim my fingers along his jawline. Stick my other hand under his shirt. "Have you told her?"

Poor Ginger. I understand what she's going through if she fell hard for Seven too.

"I spoke with her before I came here."

"How'd she take it?"

"Not well." His fingers trench in my hair. "Be my girl, Leigh."

"I can't."

"Why not?"

"It's not fair to her. Did you tell her how you felt about me?"

"Yes, Leigh. I laid it all out on the line. Confessed that I liked you from the start. Since you got off the bus that first day of school."

"Wait, you did?"

"Yes, baby."

"Seven." Jesus, when he says stupid, unexpected stuff like that, he unravels me. Tears well in my eyes. It's not right to want him so badly and agree to be his girl when he put a different girl in the position I was in, hurting and hating on him.

"Baby, please don't cry."

"I hate you."

"Still?"

"You misled me. I said we are not friends and you told me never that, never just friends."

"I didn't mislead you, babe. With us, we can never be just friends. From the day I met you and you glared back when you saw me staring, I knew I wanted to be something more to you. Except I went about it the wrong way. I told you you're mine. Told. Demanded. But never asked. Be my girl, Leigh Kim?"

How can I refuse when he wears his heart on his sleeve?

"Yes, Seven. Yes, I'll be yours."

I live in the here and now, happier than I have ever been in my life. Little did I know, my perfect world would come crashing down around me with another godawful truth that was kept from me.

"Seven, we can't seriously go rolling down the hillside. What if there's cow poop or snakes in the grass, or sharp objects?"

We stare down the hillside that ends close to the spot where Maddox dug up the safe. Seven points at the section of grass he wants us to tumble down.

"Do you see any shit or snakes or anything sharp that will poke you?"

The grass is freshly cut. Thomas had it done as

soon as I opened my mouth and suggested I be his new groundskeeper.

"No."

"Point made. Now come on. The faster we do this, the faster we can go for a bike ride. Then my parents want to meet you."

When Seven was at my place last night, his dad was with his mom. On our way up the hillside, holding hands, he filled me in. He got the text late last night. His mom invited his dad to stay over after his confession, and the rest is history. I can't wait to meet Seven's parents. Their second chance gives me hope in the power of love.

"You go first," I say.

"Promise you'll follow?"

"Wait a minute. You said you're not a follower. How about *you* follow *my* lead?"

He smiles, and coming from behind, he slips his arms around my waist and nuzzles my neck. "Gladly."

I go down the hill first, laughing all the way. I stand and sway. Goodness that was fun, but I am *dizzy*.

"Doing okay?" Seven stands, and he is completely steady on his feet.

"You've done this before," I accuse, playfully shoving my finger into his chest.

He takes my finger and strokes up and down, his eyes fixed on my mouth. "First time, honest to God."

Unable to look away from the smolder in his eyes, I tip my head up, reading him like an open book. His mouth crashes over mine. He tastes good. Morning coffee and peppermint.

His fingers shove in my hair. I lean into him. His thickness presses into my stomach, and a moan slips from me. It's embarrassing how much I want him. Or the sex noises I make when he turns me on. Moaning. Sighs full of longing. Groaning. Breathless and dizzy, I break off the kiss, and cradling his face in my hand, I tell him what I would like him to give me for a belated birthday gift.

"Leigh, are you sure?" He searches my face for clues.

"I can't wait until my next birthday. I want you to be my first, Seven Shanahan. Say yes."

He slings me over his shoulder, and with purpose in his steps, he makes his way to my place.

I take it that's a yes.

*S*he trusts me with her heart. Wants me to be her first. I'm in heaven. A lucky bastard. Inside her room, we stare at one another.

She bites down on her lower lip. Looks away. I grasp her chin and tip her face up.

"I can wait, Leigh. We have all the time in the world."

"I don't know if I'll be following you to DU. Anyway, you'll get picked for the football team. Be their next quarterback. King of the game and king on campus. You'll want a different queen. Someone prettier. Someone who falls in line and won't embarrass you or defy."

I scoff. "Believe me, looking as fine as you did at that damn party, the guys will wonder why you're with an ugly fuck like me. Live for the moment, Leigh. Let's take this a day at a time, baby."

Her eyes slide to the floor. "Okay."

Something else is wrong.

"Babe, you're my everything."

"You mean the world to me too."

She's still not looking at me.

"Then what's wrong?"

"You've only seen my scars in the dark."

Aw, shit.

I reach for the remote and hit the "on" button. The panel on the ceiling opens. It's daylight. It started raining.

"Day or night, rain or shine, you are beautiful inside and out, Leigh."

"Seven."

She looks up. Tears gather in her eyes. Her bottom lip trembles. My chest aches, knowing the hell she went through to get the scars on her body.

Which brings me to what the hell happened the day she came over and returned my lucky coin? She hadn't looked at me for a reason. Leigh was crying. What made Maddox come to Cambridge, carting Leigh off to paradise as though he were her knight in shining armor?

My temper rises, and I shove that bad shit down.

"Leigh, we can wait until dark."

"No, I'd . . . I'd like for us to make love."

"Make love. That's nice. Sounds grown up. What grown-ups do. Beats hooking up." I smile and waggle my brows, earning me a scowl from her pretty face and a smack on the shoulder.

"Seven Shanahan, you are terrible."

"I'm your terrible. All yours, Leigh." I step back and yank my shirt over my head. "Defy, babe. Give those guys who fucked you up the finger. Show them you own your defiance."

Her eyes widen. Liquid amber, and I am hard. She tips her chin. Strips off her shirt. Tosses her bra on the floor. Yanks off her pants and underwear. She stands before me in her birthday suit, a goddess with her raven hair, golden eyes, full red lips, and the scars on her smooth skin just above her sex. She is a sight to behold, my princess, my fighter, my Beautiful Defiance, and Leigh is mine.

I strip and open my arms to her. "I'm yours, baby. All yours for the taking."

Her gaze trails over my body, from my eyes to my steel abs to my erect cock. Her eyes widen. She's nervous. But that doesn't stop Leigh from looking her fill. I stand before her, not shy about putting my body on full display.

And I'm digging that she's not shy about wanting me. She licks her lips, and getting on the bed, she crooks her finger. I grab my dick and crank it side to side. It's been a long time since I've had sex, and thank fuck it's Leigh I'll be making love to.

She is everything I didn't know I wanted in a girl. She is fire and water. Hot and cold. Strong and vulnerable.

"I am yours, Leigh." I slide my body over hers, keeping my weight off her with my arms alongside her head. "I care so much for you, babe."

Her hair is a thick mass of black on her white pillowcase. Beautiful. Goddamn, she is beautiful.

"I'm yours too, Seven." She skims her fingers up and down my arms. Goosebumps rise on my skin from the feather-light caresses.

Ready to give her the world, I dip my head and kiss the corner of her mouth. "Pinky swear you'll always be mine?"

I press my mouth on hers. Her lips curve under mine.

"I pinky swear." She tongues the corner of my mouth.

I get her on a technicality. "You tongued me."

"No shit, Sherlock."

Laughter sputters from me. This girl.

"I'd like to tongue other parts of you. Especially this part." She grabs my cock. My cock thickens, hardens. Shit, is it possible to get *this* rock hard?

"You'll have to tell me if I'm doing it right, Seven. I've never, um, I've never given a guy oral."

Holy fuck, that is hot knowing I'll be her first. I kiss the fuck out of her until she is kissing me back, hard, her arms and legs wrapping around me as she tips her hip and wets my dick with her pussy juices.

"Fuck, Leigh. It's been too long. I won't last."

"How about I get you off first? Will that help you last longer next go around?"

I nod, too turned on to speak worth a damn.

"Get on your back, Seven."

Can this girl talk dirty or what? I roll off her and get on my back. She kisses me, then goes low, worshipping my six-pack abs with her tongue and her mouth. Before she gets to my cock, I need a taste of her. I'm selfish that way.

"Come here, Leigh. Put your tits in my face."

"Okay." Her mouth parts, and her eyes glaze over with lust.

Her tits hang in my face, and I take one nipple, then the other, in my mouth. Using my tongue and my teeth, I suck and graze and lick. She rocks her hips and slicks her wetness over my length. I rub her clit. Slip my finger in her heat. She's wet. Tight.

"Oh my God, Seven, that feels so good."

She sits up straight, robbing me of a view and a taste of her fine-ass tits. I groan in protest, but when she rolls her hips and moves over my cock . . . Fuck, fuck.

"Fuuuuckk."

"That feels good?"

"Hell yeah."

"I thought so." Sly grin. Mischievous gleam in her eyes. "Now I'm ready. I want a taste of us."

Oh, fuck me, this girl . . .

She moves down my body and takes my cock in her mouth. Wet. Warm. Tight. Her small mouth taking my big cock. The tip of my cock hitting the back of her throat. I come off the bed. She digs her nails into my hips. Moves them to my ass cheeks. Kneads my flesh.

Groaning, writhing, fucking writhing under the skill of her tongue and her mouth, I fist my fingers in her hair and guide her up and down my rod.

She pumps me in and out of her mouth. Takes all of my length and thickness. Pounds her mouth over my dick. Over and over.

"I . . . fuck, Leigh, I can't. I'm gonna come, babe. Let go now or I'll blow my load."

She sucks harder. Doesn't let go of her hold on my cock with her mouth or her hand. Her fingers dig into my ass cheek. Pressure uncoils in my groin. A wave of heat rolls over my body. My eyes roll back in my head, and I shoot my hot cum in her mouth.

Leigh takes it. Swallows. Wipes her mouth. I yank her up and smash my mouth over hers. Salty. Hot. I flip her onto her back. There's no resistance. Her body is lax. She's smiling. Licking her lips again.

"Mmm, you taste good."

"That so?"

"So."

"Good. My turn."

I suck on her tits. Stroke her clit. Rub the swollen nub until she cries out. Needing more of her sex noises, I slip my fingers in her heat. Pump in and out of her with one finger. Two fingers. Fuck, she is wet, tight. I groan. Enough finger fucking. I need a taste of her.

I press my face to her heat. Lick up her pussy juices. She slides up in bed. Uh-uh. I hook my arms around her thighs and pull her to me. I eat her up, eat her out. She moans. Rests her heels on my shoulders. Slides her fingers in my hair, yanking and pulling at the strands with every lick and pull of her clit from my mouth.

"Seven."

She's panting. Good. My dick comes to life again. I lick more. Suck her pussy lips into my mouth. Taste her. Will have pussy breath for the rest of the day. Won't shower until I know I'll be eating her out again.

"Seven, I want you inside me."

"Come for me first, baby."

She comes on command, and shit, my chest puffs out like I'm the rooster in the hen house. Hungry for more, I roll the condom on, slide back over her body, and nudge the tip of my cock to her opening. She wraps her legs around my waist and yanks me down to her.

"Just do it, Seven. I'm ready. More than ready."

I slide my cock inside her inch by inch. Break through her barrier. She sucks in a breath. Her body stills.

"Doing okay?"

"Better than okay."

She smiles, and that's my signal to move. I pump in and out of her, watching her face with every in and out. Is she hurting? Am I making her first time good for her?

"Seven?"

"Yes, baby?"

"Stop thinking so hard. In this, just be."

In this, just be.

In this.

Just be.

I slam into her.

Pound inside her wet pussy.

Over and over.

Her back arches.

Her legs wrap around my waist.

Make their way to my shoulders.

Holding on to her hips, I rock into her.

Her nails rake my back. Her heels dig into my shoulders.

"Harder."

"Fuck, Leigh." I grit my teeth. She is tight, wet.

"Harder, Seven."

Her inner muscles clench my rod. She opens her legs wide. Black hair fanned out around her. Smooth tan skin. Bright amber eyes. Fuck, she's beautiful, and Leigh is mine. Fucking mine.

Grunting, groaning, I pound into her. We come in an explosion of heavy breathing and skin slapping on skin, her inner muscles milking me until I am spent and slumping on her body, too sated to give a fuck that I could be crushing her.

She drags her nose over mine. Presses her mouth on mine. She is fire and defiance, and she is mine. All mine.

"I'm yours too. All yours, Seven."

I said the words out loud, and I'll be damned if I ever take them back.

I am Beautiful Defiance's guy. No doubt about that. Ever.

37

LEIGH

I didn't go over to Seven's and meet his parents. Instead, after we made love, he cleaned me up, held me in his arms, and we talked. We spoke of our dreams. Got to know one another more. I want to help kids. He would like to play football professionally.

If that dream doesn't come true, he would like to be a football coach. Someday, we would marry the two, helping kids by offering scholarships based on need, talent, or grades. Why not give the kids choices? We also talked about what a relationship would look like. Trust. Support. Listening. *Talking.*

I didn't tell him of my mom's plan to divorce my father. Why tell? It would kill off his hope that his parents' marriage will be okay after talking and making love. My parents did that too. Yet, what did it do for them other than delay the inevitable—my mom leaving my dad for her secret lover?

"Hey, doing okay?"

I blink. Seven is looking at me with a concerned expression.

"Yeah, why?"

"You were staring off into space. Ready?" He extends his hand to me. I'm sitting on the bleachers, waiting for him to be done with practice.

I set my hand in his, and he tugs me to my feet. It's mid-week, and we're back to our routine, the one we had before Seven decided I was a distraction and needed ditching for a girl who didn't do it for him.

When he was cleaning off the blood from me losing my virginity, I almost reconsidered forgiving him so quickly. I should have slammed the door in his face. Stole something else from him, like his letterman jacket. Or burned his collection of expensive sneakers. I would ignore those puppy eyes and how defeated he looked standing in front of my door with his peace offering next to his feet.

I had this burning need to have him feel what I went through. The crushing hurt and ache in my chest. My longing for his presence. The emptiness inside me knowing he'll never come through my bedroom window again.

I opened my mouth, ready to tell him I changed my mind. That I needed a good month away from him. Even that wouldn't be a guarantee I'd take him back. Except he changed my mind with the tenderness and hope on his pretty face.

"Would you mind if we plant the roses? Unless you'd rather I take them back. It was dumb of me to think you'd want red and white roses." He'd gathered me in his arms and kissed the top of my head. "A dozen roses isn't enough to show you how sorry I am, Leigh."

"No."

"No?"

"I . . . Seven, I love them. Let's go plant."

With the moon and the stars as our witnesses, he used the shovel that was on the ground, leftover from Maddox, and dug two holes.

"The colors are for you and me."

"Which one am I?"

"White. Pure, beautiful, didn't have your first kiss until you were eighteen. Red is mine. I'd bleed for you, Leigh."

Maybe so, but I would never ask him to hurt for

me or fight my battles. Alistair taught me to be independent and stick up for myself.

"Do you like sitting outside for a change?" Seven's voice pulls me back to the present.

"I do."

"I'd do you too. I mean, I do like having you sit out here too."

Sheepish grin from Seven. My attention hangs on his mouth. So sexy. He's so hot. Stinking adorable when he gets tongue-tied, which is not often. That boy, minus the f-bombs, can be so eloquent. A romantic too. And he's my guy. How is it possible a girl with nothing to her name found someone willing to give her her heart's desires?

I look at him with everything in my heart. Hope. Excitement. Anticipation. *Longing.*

"Seven." His name edges from my lips in a breathless-like whisper.

"Babe."

He steps into my space. He smells good. Sweat. The cool air. Male. I'm heady with need. He cups my face. Slides his fingers under my hair. Weaves his thick fingers in the strands and pulls me close.

"You're beautiful, Leigh. So goddamn beautiful. You're mighty fine with your arms stretched behind you and your face tipped up to the sun. Seeing you like that, it took everything in me not to run over and kiss you senseless."

"Why didn't you?" I challenge.

"Coach would've reamed me out for distracting the other players. Why, you want me to?"

My mouth is cotton dry. I run the tip of my tongue over my bottom lip. Suck my bottom lip into my mouth. Seven follows the movements. Groans. Sets his forehead on mine.

"Leigh, you're killing me, babe."

"Is that so?"

"So. Fuck," he murmurs on my mouth.

I close my eyes and inhale his scent. Relax into his body when his fingers massage my scalp.

"My dad taught me to defy, but for the right reason." I open my eyes. His are so dark. Like looking up at the sky on a moonless night.

His gaze drops to my mouth. "A kiss is a good enough reason. God, Leigh, I'll defy until the cows come the fuck home just to have all your kisses, babe."

"I want that too."

"Only with me, baby."

"Only you, Seven."

Since Seven made it clear I'm his girl, holding my hand and walking me to my classes at the start of the week, the guys who aren't his loyal teammates, who play other sports like basketball and baseball, aren't shy with their intense checking out of me. In the hallways. The cafeteria. They are wondering what the appeal is.

I get it. I'm not the prettiest girl in the school. Or a social butterfly. Or the most fashionable girl. Nor am I rich.

What does Seven see in me? The guys stare. Ask for my number. Slip me notes asking if I can tutor them too. Seven sees what's going on, and thank goodness he keeps his temper in check. There are no thrown punches. Or a garage full of expensive cars getting blown up.

It's great he's easing up on the destructive behavior, but his wanting to be with me and showing the world publicly that I'm his girl doesn't get rid of my doubts.

What if I'm a temporary fascination? What if everything he told me isn't genuine? My mother blatantly told my father she loved him, but she'd already given her heart to someone else.

As though sensing my doubts, Seven kisses me with this gut-wrenching desperation.

"You're mine, baby. Always," he says between our

kisses, his palms clasping the sides of my head. "Tell me I'm yours?"

"You're mine, Seven."

"Always?"

"Always."

Before I can say more or deepen the kiss further, there's whooping and hollering from behind us. The players have gathered around his truck. The cheerleaders hang back. Hannah gives me a cheesy grin and a double thumbs-up. Ginger is staring at the ground. Poor girl.

I place my hands on Seven's chest. "She's hurting," I say in a low voice. "Let's go easy on the PDA, okay?"

A flash of annoyance on his face. What I'm fast learning is Seven doesn't take well to policing his actions. If he had his way, he would be kissing and touching me every chance he gets.

I climb inside his truck. He runs around the truck and gets in, fist bumping Trace and Malice on the way. The guys tip their heads at me and smile. I smile back.

"Fuck, I am ready for a shower." He backs up the truck, pulls out of the school parking lot, and gets on the road.

"Don't."

"Huh?" He looks at me and raises a brow before returning his attention to the road.

"Don't shower. I want a taste of you first."

His head swivels to me. His eyes are wide. Groaning, he bounces the back of his head on the headrest.

"Shit, baby, you are dirty."

"Dirty for you."

He reaches for me. I put my hand in his and interlace our fingers.

"Leigh?"

"Hmm?"

"Will you go to homecoming with me?"

Will I? "Yes." If he wasn't driving, I would tackle him to the ground and kiss him until *his* toes curl.

"Will you be at the game?"

"Yes. Miles gave me the night off. Said no way will I miss the most important game of the season."

A game between Delridge and Cambridge.

Steering with one hand, Seven turns onto the road that will take us to our places. Instead of making a U-turn and parking alongside the fence, he stops the truck and puts it in park.

"Come on, Leigh, switch seats."

"What? Why?"

"I'm gonna teach you how to drive."

"But I lost the bet," I sputtered.

"I didn't win fair and square, baby. I'd been watching you and knew those sideline shots were your weakness."

"Seven Shanahan, to think you took advantage." I lean in and kiss him. "Thank you for telling me."

We switch seats. I shift the truck into drive and take it easy. He loves this truck, and I don't want to mess things up by crashing his baby.

"You're a natural."

Beaming, I turn onto the road that goes to his house.

"Keep going. The road dead ends at the back of the house."

"What's over there?"

"Nothing but trees."

"That's nice, Seven."

"It is. There's also a field. A great place to lay in the bed of the truck and stargaze."

"Sounds wonderful."

"Will you?"

"Will I what?" I ask, biting down on my smile.

"Stargaze with me?"

"I'd love to."

He is such a good guy. A romantic.

I take the curve slowly. He's right. There is an

open field to our right and nothing but trees to our left and ahead of us. I put the truck in park. We get out, and he picks me up and sits me on the hood.

"You did great, baby."

"I learned from the best."

He scoffs and rolls his eyes. "As if."

I laugh. "Seven Shanahan, you are stinking adorable."

"I am?"

"You know you are." I grab him by the collar of his uniform and yank him in for a kiss.

Mmm, he tastes good. Salty. Sweet. I slip my tongue inside his mouth and deepen the kiss. He groans. I suck on his tongue. Suck his bottom lip into my mouth. Nip on his lip. Tongue the corners of his mouth.

Needing him closer, I weave my fingers in his hair. The side of my face tingles. A nervous prickle slides up and down my spine. Cupping his face, I break off our kiss and look off to the side. Across the open field, my gaze locks with Sorrow's dad's. He's on the back deck, and he's holding a shotgun.

"Seven, we should go."

He looks where I'm looking. "Shit. I haven't seen him out in the open for a long ass time. Whatever he says or does, don't ever go near his place."

I cannot look away from the craze in his eyes.

"Leigh, did you hear me?"

"Yes."

"Promise?"

My defiance cost me my parents' lives. I won't let any harm come to Sorrow. I'll listen to Seven's warning and the worry in his voice.

"I promise."

What should have been one of my happiest days, a fairy tale come true, crashes and burns by the end of the night.

On the way to the homecoming dance, dressed in the dress I had crushed hard on, Seven and I argued. Our first fight as a couple.

"Why the fuck didn't you tell me you'd be sitting on our fucking opponents' side, Leigh?"

He doesn't give me time to answer.

"Do you know what that looked like to the rest of the school?"

"Rue is my friend. So is Winslow."

Winslow isn't a football player. He is into dirt biking, and is pretty good from what Rue tells me when he went off to get us drinks and hot dogs from the concession stand.

"I'm your guy. Your loyalty is to me first."

"You're making a big deal out of nothing."

"Loyalty isn't nothing."

"Friendship is a part of loyalty," I say. "They're my friends."

"Are you saying *we* aren't friends?"

"You're twisting my words," I grind out.

We don't say any more. We're at the school, and Trace and Malice are waiting for us by the front door with their dates.

"We'll talk about this later. Play nice, Leigh."

"Is that your way of telling me to fall in line? To smile and be obedient?"

He shifts in his seat and reaches for my hand. I keep my hands balled in my lap. He leans in, unfurls them, and brings my knuckles to his mouth.

"All I ask is for you not to mouth off. We won the game, Leigh. Let's celebrate, yeah?"

His face softening, he presses his mouth to my knuckles. "I care for you. So much, Defiance. Do this for me, won't you?"

What he's asking for hurts. I'm right. I don't belong in Seven's world. My urge to defy is too strong. My will to not be caged runs too deep.

Look at my mom. She involved herself with a

married man and got pregnant. Involved herself with a criminal. Had an affair and fell in love with a police officer from a powerful family. How can someone like Seven, who expects me to "fall in line" and be obedient, not be ashamed or embarrassed when my urge to defy and be disobedient rears its ugly head?

"Okay," I mumble, hating myself for giving in.

I'm also not liking the resentment growing inside me. What right does Seven have for putting limits on who I am? If he wants to be with me, he should accept me for me.

"Wait for me."

Hoping there's a hidden meaning behind his words, that maybe he'll redeem himself and stop being a jerk with this talk of loyalty and behaving myself, I do as he asks. Resting bitch face, chill-lax.

Seven gets out of the truck and hurries around to the passenger-side door. I drink him in with my eyes. Said boyfriend is acting like a grade-A jockhole currently, but I can't help admiring that his royal gorgeousness is all mine.

Seven's hair is gelled up into these delicious spikes, and he is suave in a tux that molds to his body, highlighting the parts of him I love running my hands and my mouth over.

Which is everywhere. His wide shoulders. Broad chest. Taut abs. Thick thighs. His large package. Remembering how hard he came in my mouth the day of my first driving lesson, how salty he tasted, the heady scent of sweat clinging to his hair and his thickness, my cheeks heat.

I will never tire of giving Seven oral. He makes me feel so good when he goes down on me, when he pounds into my sex, that I want to give back as much feel goods as he gives me.

The truck door opens. I slide off the seat and set my hand in his. We forget our fight temporarily and make our way inside the school and to the gym. Trace and Malice trail behind us with their dates. I recognize the girls. They're cheerleaders. Seven's court is made up of them and his teammates. They belong. I'm the outsider.

Pushing the thoughts and my doubts aside, I hand over my coat and my purse to the attendant.

While I give the attendant my information, Seven stands off to the side and looks me up and down, not being shy. Heat flashes in his eyes, and he scowls. I duck my head and hide my smile.

Poor guy. He wants me, but after the shit he gave me for being a disloyal girlfriend, he knows he'll have to kiss up big time before I hop into bed with him again.

The attendant hands me my ticket, and I give it to Seven. He puts it in his jacket pocket.

"Where's your EpiPen?"

"In my purse."

"Hand it over, Leigh. It's better to be safe than sorry."

My heart melts. Why am I having doubts when he cares enough to want to keep me safe? I ask the attendant for my purse. She hands it over. I find my EpiPen and give her back the purse.

Needing to touch and thank him for thinking of my well-being, I lean into Seven, slide my hand inside his jacket, and slip the EpiPen in the inner pocket. On the toes of my feet, I lock my lips on his. He kisses me back. We break up when the principal taps Seven on the shoulder.

"You're the best," I murmur on his mouth. "My world."

His arms wrap around me. His warm breath coasts over my mouth. Ignoring everyone around us, the principal included, Seven's mouth descends on mine, his answer buried in that kiss. I am his world too.

After what seems like minutes of a kiss that curls

my toes, we pull apart, out of breath. His eyes glaze over with desire. Mine must look like that too.

For the rest of our time, we mingle and dance. Half-way through the dance, the principal calls Seven onstage to give a speech. He goes up onstage and invites his teammates up there with him. I watch by the refreshment table with a big grin on my face. I cannot stop smiling. He is so handsome, a vision of sexiness and endless energy and enthusiasm.

"First off, thank you to my teammates for a hell of a win. You guys are the bomb. BAMFs from another mother. I am proud to call you guys my brothers for life."

"For life!" they holler.

"Second, let's give a round of applause to Ginger and her cheerleaders for supporting us on the sidelines. You girls rock with your sexy-as-fuck moves."

The principal lets Seven's f-bomb slide, and the crowd notices. They whoop and holler their approval.

"Third, thank you, all of you, for showing up and cheering us on. We couldn't have done it without you guys. Now, let's party the rest of the fucking night away!"

On cue, the music blasts. It's a fast beat worthy of

a mosh pit. My head hurting from barely eating anything—I was a nervous wreck while Eleanor and Hannah fawned over my hair and makeup—I make my way to the bathroom.

A bloom of disappointment spreads across my chest. Did I expect Seven to include me in his speech? I shouldn't. I tutored him, but Seven did the work. Still . . . I swallow past the lump in my throat. He could have mentioned his *girlfriend*.

Sitting in the stall of the bathroom, I reframe my thinking and square my shoulders. What am I thinking? I am my father's child, raised by a criminal. A girl who stole a billionaire's limited-edition sportscar. A girl who stole said billionaire's sex tapes to use as leverage. I am not going to wallow in self-pity just because my hot boyfriend didn't acknowledge my existence to a bunch of kids I couldn't care less for.

High school is but one piece of my life, of our lives. No matter what happens, Seven chose to be with me. Had asked me to be his girl. Asked me to declare him as mine too. I also have my friends.

I can always count on Maddox, Rue, Red, Winslow, Shay, Miles, and Sorrow to be there for me. Like me, they don't care what people think. They pave their own paths in life. Will forge their own futures. Those are the people who matter most, and not everyone else.

My mind made up to have fun and enjoy my time with Seven, I do my business, wash my hands, and walk straight into a nightmare.

Seven is in the hallway, swapping spit with Ginger. His mouth full on hers. Her arms wrapped tight around his neck. I see red. Hear the blood roar in my ears. I want to rip her hair out. I aim to kick him in his cheating balls. How could he? How the hell could he do this to me?

I march toward them.

Hear Seven's voice in my head. *All I ask is for you not to mouth off. We won the game, Leigh. Let's celebrate, yeah?*

He wants a girl who falls in line.

A girl who follows the rules.

Who doesn't defy.

I'm not that girl, and he can go to hell for all I care.

Tears well in my eyes and obscure my sight. Dashing at them, I stumble past Seven. He must've felt me brush up against his back as I hurried past. He calls after me. I don't stop. I keep going until I push open the double doors, the cool breeze caressing my tear-streaked face.

Why cry?

Why hurt?

I am done.

Done with believing he's changed for the better. Done with his lies and his promises. Done with being obedient and "falling in line."

Doing those things has gotten me nothing but heartache, and I hate when my heart breaks.

39

LEIGH

I shimmy the lock and jack Seven's truck.

I don't feel bad at all. Not one bit.

I can't drive worth a damn. Don't have my license. My foster family wanted to keep me in line and out of trouble. Well, here is a middle finger to them all.

I careen down the road headed for the sanctuary of my place. As soon as I get there, I'll smash the remote for the skylight into little bits and pieces, then bury those pieces next to the rose bushes after I yank the roses from the ground with my bare hands. Forget the little thorns.

After what Seven did, I'm numb to feeling anything except for anger.

I hate this town. Regret that I contacted Thomas.

Wish to God Alistair never told me the truth of who my real father is.

If he hadn't, I would be living on my own in a dingy apartment somewhere with a bunch of roommates. Being of legal age, an adult, I can do that. And stuck in that hopeless situation, I would have the motivation to be better, to climb my way out of the hole of poverty and hopelessness for someone in my predicament.

Instead, I got a taste of what money can give me and the type of guy I can be with. Someone who has a future. Who isn't addicted to drugs or drinking or considers breaking and entering a paying job. I pound on the steering wheel and blink at the tears in my eyes.

"Stupid, stupid, stupid. How could you fall for his dumb words? He only wanted in your pants. Only wanted you to give him oral."

Except he didn't just want things from me. Seven gave of himself. Shared with me his dreams and his failures. Dug a hole and planted me roses, for goodness' sake. Risked life and limb to teach me to drive, a girl who crashed a car on her first time behind the wheel. He's a good guy.

No matter what I saw, after what he believes his father put his mother through, Seven would never cheat on me. I should go back and get an explanation from him. Should've defied and made a stink, demanding to know what he was doing with his tongue shoved down Ginger's throat. I'd mouth off. I'd defy. I'd pull that bitch's hair for messing with what's mine.

I make a wide turn onto the road leading to our houses. Then I see it. Flames shooting from way up past where Seven's parents' house is. *Sorrow.*

I back up and barrel up the street. With one hand on the steering wheel, I reach for my purse. I have to call 911. My hand grazes the empty seat. Crap! I left my purse and cellphone at the dance, and Thomas and Eleanor aren't home.

I hurry up Seven's road, and not giving a care that I'll leave tire marks on the pristine field of cut grass, I step on the gas, hold on to the steering wheel for dear life, and drive across the field and straight up to the back of Sorrow's house. I shove the driver-side door open, and yelling Sorrow's name, I hike up my dress and bolt to the front of the house where the door going down to the basement is.

Sorrow stays down there to keep out of her dad's way. Out of sight, out of mind. He's a jumpy drunk, but he can also be mean and vindictive. He blames Sorrow for her mother's suicide, and every chance he gets, he reminds her that his addiction is Sorrow's fault.

What a bunch of bullshit. Sorrow is the kindest person.

"Sorrow! Sorrow, let me in!" I bang on the door. Last time I was here was for Sorrow's birthday. She'd answered right away.

There's none now. Worried, I twist the doorknob and pull. The door doesn't budge.

I bolt for the front door. The barrel of a gun shoved against the back of my head stops me.

"Get in the house, now." Sorrow's dad's words are slurred, and there is a distinct smell on his breath and his clothes. Alcohol and pot.

"Sorrow—"

"I said get in the house."

Sorrow's dad shoves me toward the back of the house. His shoves are forceful, and I fall forward, tripping on the steps of the back deck. He rights me, stopping me from faceplanting. His fingers dig into my arm.

The door opens. Sorrow is on the other side. Her face twists into an expression of terror when she sees me, her dad, and the gun.

"Leigh." She rushes to me.

Her dad waves his gun. She stops.

"Dad, please, let Leigh go."

He tightens his hold on my arm. "Did you give my daughter a connection to the outside world?"

"Yes," I admit. "Sorrow needs a lifeline. A way to get you help." Sorrow would never have the nerve to ask her father for a cellphone.

"We don't need you meddling in our lives."

"Sorrow needs friends and a life of her own. You can't keep punishing her for something she isn't responsible for. Your wife was deeply depressed. You need help with your drinking. Please. I can help you and Sorrow."

"We don't need your goddamn help! We were fine before you broke into our place."

"I didn't break in. I heard Sorrow crying. She let me in. We talked."

The fire is burning faster and hotter on the other side of the door. We're in a different room of the house. What used to be an office before it was gutted and emptied of every piece of furniture. There is nothing in here but moving boxes.

"Please, Mr. Sophia, we need to call 911."

"You ain't calling anyone. Open the damn door."

"The fire—"

"Open the damn door!"

I can't. If I do, it'll be the death of us.

"No."

"What did you say?"

"No. You will hand over your gun and get yourself help. You owe Sorrow that. You took away three years of her life."

Sorrow's dad told everyone Sorrow ran away.

Pissed at him for the lie and sad for Sorrow, I shove my elbow into his gut and come down hard on his shin with the point of my high-heel shoe.

He cries out. I pivot and pull back my arm, ready to nail him again. Something hard jams into the side of my head. A cracking sound fills my ears. My world spins. I crash to the ground.

"Leigh! Leigh!"

Sorrow's voice comes to me as though from a distance.

Dazed, I blink and stare up at the white ceiling. Heat sears one side of my body. Groaning, I glance off to the side. The office door is open. Sorrow and her dad are in the middle of the burning room. I push onto my feet and stagger after them. He has a gun pointed at Sorrow's head. Oh, God, it was my fault. I gave her the phone. My fault that he found out and is so angry.

I can't let it end like this. I take a step, and another.

"Please, let her go. Hurt me instead."

I stretch out my hands, palms up, imploring, begging him to let her go. Tears blur my vision.

"No one needs to know what happened here. It'll be our secret. Please. She's my friend."

Something in him changes. The craze in his eyes fades, the haze of his drunkenness and his high momentarily replaced with clarity.

"You'll make sure she's taken care of?"

"Yes." I step closer. He backs up toward the flames.

"Leigh! Leigh, are you in there?"

Seven? And there are sirens and commotion on the other side of the front door. Over Sorrow's dad's shoulders, I see my guy. The look of sheer horror and panic on his face.

Sorrow's dad raises the shotgun, drawing my attention back to him and Sorrow. This is it. This is it. Uttering a wish and a prayer that we make it out of this alive, I charge him the same time Sorrow twists out of his hold.

"I love you, Sorrow. I'm so sorry, sweetheart. Take care of her, Leigh."

The gun goes off. Mr. Sophia tips to the side and crumples to the floor. The roof caves in, the fire having started on the top floor. I reach for Sorrow.

She puts her hand in mine. We close our eyes. The heat is unbearable. I choke on the smoke. This is it. Eighteen years of living going up in flames and smoke.

Robbed of breath, my lungs filling with smoke, I close my eyes and give in to the darkness.

*H*er eyes flutter open, and I heave a sigh of relief.

"Leigh, baby." I clasp her head in my palm and lay a kiss on her forehead. "Goddamn, you scared the fuck out of me."

We are back at the hospital. Both Leigh and the girl in the burning house with her suffered smoke inhalation. The doctors kept them overnight for observation to be on the safe side.

The oxygen mask is off her face, and she now has these prongs in her nostrils giving her a smaller dose of oxygen. I'm expecting her to ream me out for that damn kiss, but of course, Leigh isn't predictable.

"My friend Sorrow? Is she okay? Her father. What happened to her father?"

Sorrow, the girl with long black hair and the deepest blue eyes set in a dainty face is the shy girl her father claimed ran away at fifteen. Happened after her mom overdosed. To think she's been living in that house right under our noses. I bet her "running away" had to do with her dad's fucked-up mind and drinking himself to oblivion.

"She's good, babe. They have her in the next room. Smoke inhalation. What you have too."

"Her dad?"

"He killed himself, Leigh. I'm sorry."

She bunches the covers in her hand, a single tear sliding down her face. "What will happen to her? I should ask Thomas if she can stay with me or in his place. I doubt Sorrow will want the couch. Or I can crash on the couch and she can have the bed. She'll love the skylight."

I silence her concern for her friend with my mouth pressed on hers. She kisses me back, her soft sigh of contentment the best sound I've heard in a long time. We break off our kiss, and I hold her hand, needing to touch her. For her to know I'm here and will always be here for her.

"Leigh, Trace's parents already spoke with Sorrow and offered their guesthouse to her. They told Dad and I it was their fault Kyle ended up the way he did. Trace's dad and Kyle were partners. Something happened between them, and Trace's dad ended the partnership."

I wipe the tear from her cheek. Cup her face in my palms. Her eyes close, and she utters the words I knew were coming the moment she saw me and Ginger.

"I hate you, Seven."

"I know, baby."

She opens her eyes, and I love the hardened defiance in their amber depths.

"When I saw you kissing Ginger, I wanted to steal your letterman jacket, toss all your expensive shoes out the window and set them on fire. Then I would use condoms like water balloons and chuck them inside your bedroom."

"You still can, Leigh. Use me as target practice too, baby. Or you can kick me in the balls and send your friend M after me. Go right on ahead. I deserve it. But don't take away our pinky swears. I live for those."

"Pinky swear I can use you for target practice."

"Do I stand in one place or will I be a moving target?"

"I have great aim. Am a fast runner too. The fun is in the chase, isn't?" She smirks.

I shake my head. This girl. I kiss the corner of her mouth. "We are on for a game of dodge cock sock."

She chuckles. "Nice. I love it."

Her laughter dies down and she gets all serious.

"Seeing you with her hurt, Seven. I hated you so much. But after what happened with your parents, I don't believe you would cheat on me. What'd Ginger do? When I get out of here, she's going to get a face full of cornstarch in every color of the rainbow."

"That's my girl. My spitfire." Smiling, I capture her mouth in mine. She sucks on my bottom lip. Tangles her tongue with mine. She's sweet and warm, and after she's feeling better, I intend on showing her who I belong to until we both can't walk straight.

"Leigh—" Blowing out a breath, I tent her hands and rest my forehead on them.

What I am about to tell her will hurt her, and I never want to hurt Leigh. But I want her love more than I hate hurting her, so this is my selfishness coming out to play.

"Leigh, it was stupid of me to let Ginger corner me and catch me off guard with that damn kiss. She threatened to get up onstage and broadcast the truth of why you're in Cambridge living in Thomas's guesthouse. She hired a P.I. He found a paternity suit drawn up by a lawyer you hired with the little money your parents left you. Except the suit didn't go through. Thomas moved you here in exchange for you dropping the suit. Leigh, Thomas isn't your father."

"That's right. I'm not, Leigh."

I turn toward the door. On the other side of the partially opened curtain is Thomas, along with his wife, Eleanor, and Hannah and Henry. Leigh's friends are behind them, as well as Malice and Trace.

They crowd into the room. Leigh's eyes water. She shoves her fist against her mouth. My girl is hurting, and done with seeing her hurting, I climb into bed with her and set her on my lap. I wrap my arms around her and tell her what she means to me.

"I love you, Leigh. I don't give a shit that Thomas isn't your dad. That your dad is a criminal and your mother was ready to leave him for my uncle, Tony. You're my Beautiful Defiance, and that's enough for me."

The guys, her friends, and her "family" hear me loud and clear. They chime in with their words of love and encouragement.

"Family isn't all about blood, Leigh," Thomas says with a big smile on his face. "Your parents taught me that. Yes, your mother worked for me when she was young, only seventeen, her first job at a factory I owned in Oakland. Eleanor and I were married and going through some rough times."

He sits on the chair I vacated. Eleanor follows and sets her hand on his shoulder as though saying, "Go on. Tell her the truth."

After making sure Leigh was taken care of by the hospital staff, I confronted Thomas about what Ginger said. That bitch is vindictive. I thought I had learned my lesson from a different girl who accused my father of being an arrogant ass who only wanted to see me with a girl whose family has money, but I hadn't.

Never again will I make the mistake of dropping my guard, not when it comes to Leigh and the ones who want to cause a rift between us. I also won't be misleading a different girl in, oh, never. Leigh is it for me.

When Ginger told me of her plan to get me to break things off with Leigh or she'll get up onstage and expose Leigh's life back in Cali, I was on the verge of telling her to fuck off. I opened my mouth. She grabbed me by the back of my head and slammed her mouth on mine. Stuck her tongue down my throat.

Then I felt before I saw my girl. The look on her

face. She hurt, and I wanted to shake Ginger and yell at her for fucking up Leigh's night, but I had already done that when I basically called Leigh a disloyal girlfriend. Then I fucked up more when I didn't thank her for helping me pass my classes.

Shit, I'm a clueless, ungrateful bastard, unworthy of being Beautiful Defiance's guy. Blowing out a breath, I drop kisses on the back of Leigh's hand. I'll make it up to her. Apologize until I'm out of breath. Stargaze with her every chance I get. Continue to teach her how to drive. Let her have a go at me with rounds of PIG or HORSE or whatever damn animal she chooses to play hoops to.

As though she understands what all I'll be doing for and with her, Leigh relaxes into me, and we listen to Thomas's side of the story of why he withheld the truth from Leigh.

"Your mother started dating Alistair while working for me. She didn't approve of your father's *extracurricular* activities."

I smirk. It was Leigh's father's extracurricular activities that brought in extra money for the family until Alistair straightened his life for love.

"We can't help who we fall in love with. Your mom fell in love and had you with Alistair. Then she fell out of love and into love with Tony."

The other news Ginger dropped on me. My uncle, Tony, had an affair with Leigh's mother and was planning on marrying her as soon as her divorce went through.

Except Alistair found out about the affair, hauled his wife and daughter to the police station, and in confronting my uncle, got himself and his wife killed in front of Leigh. My uncle died three years later in the line of duty, answering a domestic violence call.

"You knew all along I wasn't your daughter."

"Yes, Leigh."

Thomas runs his palm over his face, looking like he's aged a decade in the span of a minute.

"I would've told you the truth from the get-go, but I knew what you went through in those foster homes. I read the files. You needed to trust me first. To learn to open yourself to new people and experiences. To learn to let down your guard and let good people in while telling the bad ones to shove off. Had you come to me soon after your parents died, I would have given you the truth. But the girl you were at thirteen was different from the woman you are now."

Dismay. Disloyal. Destruction. Disillusioned. The backward Ds tatted at the base of her neck. She'd been and seen all of that and more.

"The dress, I bought it with the monthly allowance you put in my account. I'll pay you back. Can pack up my bags and leave as soon as I get—" She smooths the hand I'm not holding over her hospital gown. "I'll leave as soon as I get to your guesthouse."

Thomas, thank fuck, corrects and reassures her. "The place is yours, Leigh. And no need to leave. Stay. You're family."

She shakes her head. "The money—"

"Repay me if it makes you feel better. I hear the shop will need someone on a permanent basis. Mason stopped by the hospital. You were still out of it. He says the gal isn't coming back from maternity leave."

She smiles. "That was nice of him to come by."

"He cares, Leigh. We all do. We're your family now. Will you stay?"

She nods, her amber eyes shimmering with fresh tears. "Thank you, everyone. You're such good people."

"Hey, since we're all about telling truths, we should shed light on what happened to Allison," Trace pipes up from the back of the room.

"Yeah, maybe then you won't hate my cousin so much, Seven." Malice walks over and stands next to the bed. "Ginger gave Allison the drink. John did the assaulting. It was dark, and she thought it was Red. Red was the last guy she spoke to. You weren't at the party, and Red knew that. He warned Allison to keep an eye on her drink. Would've stuck around, but we had a family emergency."

That's right. Their grandmother fell and was taken to the hospital. Those Sterling guys love the fuck out of their grandmother.

"The cops have Ginger and John in custody," Malice says. "Girls from Cambridge and Delridge are coming forward. Some as recently as Brody's party."

The one where I caught that fucker Shay with his hand in my girl's hair.

"Allison warned us Ginger might do something to you or Leigh. We followed her, and bam, she didn't disappoint. But you, bro—" Malice smacks me upside the head. "Shit, you better wash your mouth with soap and water before you go kissing on our friend Leigh."

I shake my head, unable to stop smiling. "Want me to do that, baby?"

"Uh-uh. Kiss. Now." She shifts on my lap, and cocooning my head in her palms, she pulls me to her.

Thank fuck everyone has the good sense to book it out of the room and give us privacy.

Closing my eyes, I take in how soft her lips are. How nicely we fit, her ass nestled on my crotch. How randy my dick gets when she squirms when I deepen the kiss, missing her flavor, her soft sighs of contentment as she holds onto me tight with her arms wrapped around my neck. The desperate way she kisses and holds me reminds me of my own desperation as I bolted after her last night.

To think I almost lost Beautiful Defiance first to Ginger's jealousy then that damn fire. I break off the kiss.

"Leigh?"

"Hmm?"

"Can I ask you something?"

"Always."

"That night I stayed over, after we got home from the hospital, how'd you end up on the couch on top of me the next morning?"

"You had a nightmare."

"You heard me?"

"I'm a light sleeper."

"What'd you hear?"

"That you were sorry you didn't save me in time. You thought I'd drowned."

"You kissed me."

"Yes. With as much as you were hurting, you were deserving of my first kiss."

"Aw, babe." I pull her to me and clamp my mouth on hers. God, I'm one lucky bastard. I kiss her breathless. After we end the kiss and catch our breath, I tell her about Meisa. I owe Leigh the reason I didn't like her defiance.

"I'm so sorry, Seven."

"If I was a better swimmer, I could've saved her."

"Could've. Should've. You can't change the past. You can only move forward. If you want, I can teach you how to swim. I'm thinking Thomas won't mind if we use his pool."

"As long as we can swim at night and stargaze, I am in."

"I'm looking forward to it." She cradles my face in her small palm. "Thank you for saving my life last night, Seven."

"And you'll be owing me, 'cause we both know you're not in the business of owing someone you want leverage over or care for. Am I spot on, Leigh?"

"You're onto me, big guy. Will you let me even the score?" she murmurs on my mouth, her lips soft and warm.

"You already have."

Her brows furrow. "I haven't stolen anything other than your truck."

"You stole more than my truck, beautiful. Every time I'm with you, you steal pieces of my heart."

"Would you like the pieces back?" Wistful smile on her face, and I am falling harder for Beautiful Defiance.

"No, baby. My heart is yours for as long as you want me."

"A long time, Seven. I love you."

"I love you too, Leigh."

EPILOGUE

*S*even and I walk hand in hand up the road. The music from the house at the end of the road is loud. As it should be at a "happening" party.

Our friends are at Brody's party, waiting for us to show our faces. Seven and I would have been here sooner, but we had "business" to take care of. My oh my, what that boy can do with his mouth and the package in his pants.

I'm not bad myself. Seven came twice. Once in my mouth and once inside me. We cannot get enough of one another.

In non-Seven news, it's been a week since the fire. Sorrow has moved into the guesthouse on Trace's parents' property. Seven asked Trace how that's working out. I asked Sorrow the same. When Seven and I compared notes, the findings weren't good. Trace and Sorrow are not getting along.

No surprise there. Sorrow is quiet and reserved. Trace is quiet, but his quiet isn't reserved but in your face. He has this presence about him that's hard to ignore. Strong. Obstinate. A beautiful creature on the outside but something darker on the inside.

I'm crossing my fingers those two come to a compromise. Seven and I are not in the business of breaking up fights between our friends.

Speaking of fighting and friends, Rue got a job working for Malice's family. He's not on track to graduating and is causing a lot of trouble now that football season is over. Malice's family hired Rue to "babysit" Malice. The kicker? She'll be living with him in his house on his parents' property. Wow.

That's another fight Seven and I won't be breaking up. Those two have issues, and I have a feeling their hatred for one another has been coming to a head for quite some time now.

At one of our shopping trips, minus Red, I asked Rue why she hates Malice, but mum is the word from that girl.

"Hey, fucker, what's up?"

Shay marches over and smacks Seven on the

shoulder. Bypassing Seven's glare, he pulls me in for a hug.

"Glad you're alive, short stuff."

"Me too. How was your date for homecoming?" I slip my hand in Seven's and lean into him. I love this guy so much, and I want the rest of the world to know he is mine and I am his.

"A total fail. She ditched my ass. But it's my fault." He cups the back of his neck. "I came on too strong. Scared her with my loud mouth."

"Don't look now, but she's checking you out," I say, smiling.

"What? She is?" He pivots and looks in Blair's direction. Blair's face turns a shade of pink. "Fuck, what should I do?"

"Talk to her. Show her a magic trick."

"Yeah, a magic trick. Cool. See you later, Leigh." He leaves, then backtracks, facing us again. "I forgot to tell you this, fucker, but Leigh sitting on Delridge's side is my doing. In exchange for not pressing charges against your short-fused ass for knocking me on my ass, she agreed to cheer for me at the homecoming game and go to the dance with me. Except your girl got me to man up and ask out the girl of my dreams. Leigh is good people. I hope you didn't give her a hard time. She has your back."

"Thanks for telling me. I wouldn't have known." He plants a kiss on the top of my head. "Sorry, babe, for giving you a hard time. Next time, kick me in the balls, yeah? And sorry, bro, for punching you in the face multiple times. Won't happen again."

"We're good?"

"All good." They fist bump and do this explosion thing with their fingers. I shake my head. Boys will be boys.

"Will you do that, Leigh?" He pulls me against him, and we walk hip to hip to the party house.

"Kick you in the balls? Nope. I happen to like your impressive package, balls included."

"Thank fuck, because I change my mind."

Suddenly, I'm staring at the ground and we are headed back down the road.

"Seven?"

"I love you, Beautiful Defiance. Let me show you all the ways I love you."

"Can I defy?"

"Hell yeah. Your defiance turns me the fuck on."

"And your love makes me happy. You make me so happy, Seven. I love you."

My father taught me to defy. Always for the right reason. Love is as good enough of a reason.

ACKNOWLEDGMENTS

I want to take the time to thank my beta readers, Anna and Aleena. The feedback you provide is invaluable and much appreciated! I've incorporated your feedback into the story :). Thank you. Thank you. Thank you. Thank you.

x.o.
A.M.

9 781393 225355